The

Walls

Remember

Sadie Horton

979-8-9886165-8-0

The walls kept what the record could not.
Brick is a slow witness,
but it is still a witness.
They were here.
The building remembered them.
Someone finally came to listen.

CHAPTER ONE

Arrival

Day 1, afternoon

"…whatever walked there, walked alone."
— Shirley Jackson, The Haunting of Hill House (1959)

The bars were still up.

Kate brought the Outback around the last bend in the access road and Marston Hill came at her through the walnut trees: the central administration intact, the west wing slumped at one corner from the '96 storm, the east wing rebuilt once in 1923 and still wearing on its upper floors the wrought iron 1873 had bolted to the windows of the women's ward. Four on the second floor. Six on the third. Painted four times in a hundred and fifty-three years. Never once removed.

She slowed at the gate. Coasted. Killed the engine.

The padlock on the chain-link wasn't engaged yet. That was a thing she had asked the contractor to do. A site that was locked from the moment she arrived was a site that meant business. The lock was the size of her fist, brass, a Master 410 three years old by the wear on the keyway. She approved.

She got out. The wet October air found her at the wrists where the heated vest under her jacket did not reach, and she pulled the cuffs down. She stood beside the car for the count of ten and let the smell reach her. Wet leaves. Old brick. Ironwork rusting in a wet October. Underneath those three the smell every closure-eve building had, which was the smell of a hospital with the patients gone and the cleaning staff not yet come. She had done six of these. She wasn'tt sentimental about smells.

The TB sanatorium in the Adirondacks had smelled of asbestos powder twenty years after the last patient. The Berkshire prison had smelled of bleach and a thing she had never identified. The orphanage outside Hartford had smelled of pine, of all things, like a Christmas tree lot in March. Marston Hill smelled of itself.

A man was coming down the slope toward the gate. Steel-toes, black canvas jacket with the contractor's logo stitched across the chest, hard hat in his right hand. He raised the hand as he came. Calm walk. Twenty years of it.

"You'll be Welton."

"Welton. Kate."

"Mendez. Ray."

The handshake was a foreman's, dry and brief with no theatre. He glanced once at her car and read the equipment in the back seat the way men in his trade read equipment, which is quickly and without comment.

"How was the drive."

"Clear."

"You've done these."

"Seventh."

"Seventh asylum?"

"Seventh closure-eve. Three asylums. Two prisons. A school for the deaf and a TB sanatorium."

"Sanatoria are easier."

"They had windows for a reason."

He almost smiled but said nothing.

He hooked the lock back through the chain, loose, and led her along the inside of the fence. He covered the protocols as they walked, the way a foreman who had done a lot of walk-ins did them. Hard hat at all times within the fence. High vis at all times within the fence. Steel-toes he was grateful to see she already had on. Medical kit in the foreman's trailer, which was the white double-wide twenty meters east of the front entrance. The field office, by previous arrangement with the state, was the administrator's office at the back of the central building's ground floor. Potable water was in the trailer; not the building. Restrooms likewise.

"Wreckers staged Friday for a Monday start," he said. "Weather permitting."

"What's coming."

"Nor'easter. Wednesday."

"Forecasters."

"Disagree on Thursday."

She nodded. Filed both for the schedule. October weather at this latitude was, in her experience, a series of consecutive opinions.

They came around the west elevation. The building came clear through the trees as most Kirkbrides did, which was the trick of them. Enormous from the front. Modest from the side. Wings angled away from the central administration, so no patient corridor was longer than a hundred feet and no ward shared a wall with another. The architecture was an argument about care. Marston Hill had been making the argument and failing since 1873.

The west wing was original brick, three stories, slate roof with a corner spalled and the trusses underneath partly given up after the '96 storm. The central administration was three stories of pale brick with a four-column portico and a copper-trimmed cornice gone to the same green as the chapel roof beyond it. The east wing was 1923 reconstruction over the 1873 footprint. Different fire, different clay, the seam between the original masonry and the rebuild running from foundation to cornice in a single vertical line the masons of '23 had not even pretended to disguise. It was visible at fifty yards. The building's autobiographical sentence in two colors of brick, the sentence being:

they tore me down and put me back together and pretended they had not.

"East wing first," Kate said. "I want to see the bars."

"Mostly took those off in '78."

"They took them off the lower floors."

"Huh." He scratched his jaw. "That's right."

They walked counterclockwise along the perimeter. They passed the gatehouse, whose 1873 oak door was still hung on its original strap hinges. Noted the foundation outline of the water tower decommissioned in '91, demolished in '04. There was a stand of beech that had grown through a hand-laid stone retaining wall in a way that, structurally speaking, was going to take the wall down by 2035. Kate noted the wall as was her habit.

They came around to the east wing's long elevation and when she stopped on the access path with her boots a foot inside the fenceline.

The bars were 1873 wrought iron. They had been painted, once, the same flat institutional gray as the stone sills, but the gray paint went, exhausted after forty years of failing. Someone in the eighties had painted over them, less successfully.

Kate counted four windows on the second floor that still wore bars. Six on the third. The lower floors had been unbarred in '78, as Ray said, and the four bar-anchor scars per window remained, neatly patched in mortar slightly newer than the brick around it and slightly older than her career.

She raised the Pentax. She had loaded the long lens that morning at the motel.

Twelve exposures of the elevation, walking three paces sideways between each, parallax for the photogrammetric reconstruction her laptop would do that night. Four stills close on the patched scars. Two of the brick seam between '73 and '23. One of the cornice line where the iron flashing was lifting away from the parapet. She would flag that for Ray as a hazard before he sent anyone up the wall on a lift. She lowered the camera.

"Bars," she said.

"Bars," Ray said.

She nodded. They moved on.

He took her up the four shallow steps of the portico and unlocked the central door with a key from the ring on his belt loop. He leaned his shoulder into it because the jamb had settled, then stepped aside to let her go in first. She liked that. They were going to work together well.

The smell inside intensified the smell from the gate tenfold. Wet brick. Iron. The dust of a climate-control system that had been off since 2022 and whose interior had had two and a half years to make peace with the exterior. Light in the foyer was October light through dirty leaded glass. A walnut staircase rose to the left, hand-rubbed and oiled once and ignored for fifty years. The banister had a soft sag at the third newel where 153 years of elbows had worn it. The administrator's office was at the back of the ground floor, second door on the right. She had remembered this from the floor plan. She let her eye confirm it before her feet moved.

"Field office?"

"Field office."

"Duplicate keys are on your windshield. Big one's the front door. Little one's the side off the east. Ring marked Five is the basement. The hydrotherapy basement is under another lock I don't have the key to."

"Eleanor Ross has it."

He looked at her. Mildly surprised.

"You did your homework."

"I did the registry call sheet. She's on it."

"Eighty-one. In town. She'll talk to you on a good day."

"What kind of day will tomorrow be?"

He almost smiled again. "I don't know what kind of days she has anymore. I know she had them at one point."

He went out toward the trailer.

Kate stood for a moment in the foyer. Buildings said things to her. This was not a romantic claim. Twenty years of this work and she had learned to read a corridor the way other people read a face: where the wear was and was not, what had been added, what had been taken out, what the air did. The administration building of Marston Hill said:

I've been left alone, and I am tired, and there are things under the plaster.

That part wasn't unusual. They all said that.

Her phone buzzed in her jacket pocket.

She took it out.

Mom.

The first call had come at six that morning, while Kate was still in the motel outside Pittsfield. Margaret had wanted to know if she was coming for dinner. Kate had said no, she was working in another state. Margaret had said yes of course, sweetheart, and let her go. The second came at the BP off Route 8. Margaret had wanted to know if she was coming for dinner. Kate had said the same thing. Margaret had said yes of course, sweetheart. This was the third call.

The screen rang seven times. On the eighth it went to voicemail.

She put the phone back in her pocket.

Why she had not answered was a thing she would examine later. Later.

She went out to the car for her gear. Ray had left the keys on the windshield under the wiper, three on a brass ring with a paper tag in his block-letter handwriting: WELTON / SURVEY. She clipped them to the carabiner on her belt loop and unloaded what she would need for the first afternoon. Laptop. Second tripod. The long roll of mylar she used for tracing. The infrared camera in its padded case. Two boxes of nitrile gloves. The heated lap blanket she used for sitting work in a stuff sack the size of a loaf of bread. Two spare M12 batteries for the vest under her jacket, charged that morning at the motel and stowed in a foam-lined case. She left the rest. A vehicle parked at a closure-eve site for fourteen days became, over those fourteen days, a kind of remote office, and she had learned not to move too much into the building all at once.

The administrator's office was twelve by fourteen. There was oak panel to the chair rail with plaster above. She had one south-facing window onto what had been the kitchen garden and was now a meadow of dock and chicory. The original desk had gone in '94. Bookshelves seemed intact. There were outlets on each of the four walls which she tested with a penlight. Three carried current from the generator. She set up against the wall with the most reliable of the three. Then she laid the floor plans on the bare floorboards in three squared stacks. 1873 originals. 1923 reconstruction. 1947 expansion plan.

Three forty-five.

Ninety minutes of usable light left.

She found Ray outside the trailer with a thermos open on the step, smoking, holding the cigarette away from her as she approached.

"Tomorrow morning let's do a walk-through. Slowly. Both wings. Two hours minimum, four if you have it."

"I have it."

"And I'll be on-site at first light."

"How early."

"Six twenty. Civil twilight."

"You serious?"

"I'm always serious about light."

He looked at her, looked at the building, looked at her again.

"Welton."

"Mendez."

"You're going to be on this site dawn to dark for fourteen days."

"Dawn to dark."

He took a slow pull off the cigarette and exhaled away from her. "Alright then."

She went back in. There was an hour and a quarter of usable light, and there was the only thing that had to be done before dark on the first day of any closure-eve survey, which was to walk the building once, alone, and let it know she was there. She had learned from her favorite professors that buildings are alive and she chose not to question that sentiment.

The east wing's lower floor was empty and dry. The rooms were small, smaller than the original 1873 plan made them out to be, in the way only a 1923 reform-era reconstruction of a women's wing could be made easier to lock. The west wing's lower floor was empty and not dry. She found a shallow pool of standing water at the south end where the slate had failed two winters ago. She marked it on her tablet. She did not go upstairs in either wing. She would do the upstairs with Ray in the morning, when his presence would be the thing that signaled to whatever she was going to find that she had not come unaccompanied.

She went into the records room at the south end of the rear corridor. It had a plaster ceiling with dropped acoustic tile fallen in two places. There were file cabinets standing along the long wall, the kind the state had bought by the gross in the seventies, painted institutional green, drawers labeled in faded sharpie. ADMISSIONS 1968–1972. ADMISSIONS 1973–1978. DISCHARGE 1923–1928, on the cabinet at the south end, set against the wall like the others, paper still in the slot from a label that had been there long enough to fade twice. One drawer hung half open at the south end. She nudged it shut with her boot. It went home with the same dry click eighty thousand drawers like it had always made. The records room had been the records room since 1947. The records had left in 1994. The cabinets had stayed because the state did not pay to remove what nobody would buy.

She came back to the foyer at four forty-five and stood with her hand on the banister and looked up at the second-floor landing. The window above admitted, at this hour in October, a long bar of low light. The bar fell across the landing and onto the wall above and lit the wall the dirty gold of a building not used since spring.

There was nothing on the landing. Nothing on the wall. The light was simply doing what light did in a building of this orientation at four forty-five on the twenty-eighth day of October.

She stood there for a moment. Then another. Then she went out to the portico.

The sun was going down behind the west wing.

The shadow of the chapel had run forty yards into the meadow. The bar of light over the cornice flashing flared once and went out as the sun dipped below the building facade. The wind across the meadow had come up while she was inside. It went around the corners of the central administration, found nothing to do and moved on.

The meadow had been mown within the last month. The state did this at all of its closure-eve sites because the first lawsuit it had ever lost on a closure site had been about a cluster of unmown tick grass and a contract worker's daughter. Beyond the meadow, she could see the road back to the highway. Beyond the road, a stand of red maples already half stripped by autumn winds. Beyond that, the sky was the color of wet tin and getting darker. A single crow lifted from the cornice of the west wing and said nothing as it crossed the meadow at a long diagonal and was gone.

Her phone, in her jacket pocket, did not ring. Margaret made three calls a day. After three Margaret was, by some private arithmetic of her diminishing day, satisfied.

Kate stood on the portico.

The west wing's silhouette took the last of the sun.

Inside, in the administrator's office at the back of the ground floor, three stacks of blueprints waited under the south window for a woman to come back and read them.

She came back.

CHAPTER TWO

First night

Day 1, evening

"Whatever hour you woke there was a door shutting."
— Virginia Woolf, "A Haunted House" (1921)

She made the field office habitable the way she had learned to make field offices habitable. This was accomplished by treating it as a room she would have to live in, not a room she happened to be working in. The folding table came in from the car and went under the south window. The laptop on the table. The infrared camera in its padded case in the corner where no one would step on it. She placed the Pentax on the windowsill, where the late light could reach it. The blueprints came up off the floor and onto the table in three squared stacks. The chair was a Helinox Chair One she had bought in 2014, gone slack in the seat. It was, she suspected, the longest commitment she had made to any object in her apartment. She set it at the height she preferred then plugged in the laptop.

Next came the warming gear. The HVAC had been off since 2022. Her tablet, set to log ambient temperature continuously, said the administrator's office was sixty-one degrees. It would be fifty-eight by midnight. She had learned, on the third of these contracts, that you dressed to sit still, not to walk around. She turned the heated vest up from low to medium, swapped a fresh M12 into the controller in the inside pocket, and shook the lap blanket out across the back of the chair where her shoulders would meet it.

The building settled around her in the way buildings settle at dusk, which was the same way they had settled at every dusk since their construction. It took a long architectural exhale through the joists. She noted a brief small protest from the stairs. Then, a series of snaps in the radiators that had been off since 2022 and which still snapped, occasionally, like organisms remembering they had been alive.

She took the phone out of her jacket pocket and set it face up on the table.

The jacket came off and was hung on the back of the chair. She pulled the lap blanket down off the chairback and over her knees.

She sat down.

First, she listened to the voicemail.

Margaret's voicemail at three forty-one had been recorded, by the time stamp, in her own kitchen. Kate could tell by the acoustic. Margaret's kitchen had a specific resonance: galley-shaped, hard surfaces, a refrigerator on the long wall whose compressor was slightly out of round. The compressor was audible behind Margaret's voice for the first few seconds of the message.

"Kate," Margaret said. "Kate. There's a … I don't know who has been …"

A pause. The compressor shifted in pitch.

"There's a woman on the answering machine. I just listened to it. She sounds like … she sounds a great deal like me. She sounds older than I sound. I think someone has been recording over the message and putting in their own. I don't know whether to call the company or … and I don't know whether … I think someone has been moving the kitchen chairs. The chair by the window is on the wrong side of the table. I moved it back. But I had moved it. I had already moved it. Kate? Are you coming for dinner? Joanne said you were coming for dinner. Sweetheart? Call me back."

The message was a minute and seven seconds. Kate listened to it twice. Then she set the phone back on the table, face up, and did not call her mother back.

She set it down. Picked it up. Set it down again. Considered, briefly, the question of why a person picked up an object once they had decided to put it down and filed it for later in the section of her head reserved for the questions that did not have answers.

She would call her mother back tomorrow. She would not call now. The neurology of the woman who had recorded the message at three forty-one was not the neurology that would answer the phone at six. Kate had learned this over the past six months. There was a Margaret who would be relieved to hear from her, and a Margaret who would not understand who was calling, and the second Margaret was capable of sitting in a kitchen chair with the phone at her ear for an hour after the call ended, and the first Margaret was the only one whose distress Kate had any way to mitigate. She would try to do it at the part of the morning when Margaret's mind was at its most reliable, which according to Joanne's three-week journal was between nine fifteen and ten. She would call at nine thirty.

The voicemail had said: *the woman on the answering machine sounds like me, but older.*

The voicemail had been recorded in Margaret's own voice.

Kate did not, sitting at the table in the administrator's office at Marston Hill State Hospital sixteen days before its scheduled demolition, allow herself to follow that thought any further than one sentence.

She picked up the phone, pulled up Joanne, and called.

Joanne picked up on the second ring.

"You got there."

"I got there."

"And."

"It's a building, Jo."

"Kate."

"It's a Kirkbride. East wing 1923 over 1873. West wing original. Central administration intact through demo per federal survey. I'm in the administrator's office. The contractor seems competent."

"Kate. She called you three times today."

"I answered the first two."

"She called me four times."

Joanne kept a journal of Margaret's days. They were color-coded the way Joanne color-coded everything: green for stable, yellow for off, red for what she called episodes, the kind that needed to be logged and reviewed and, on the bad days, reported to the on-site director in person. Today had three reds before noon: the wandering chair, the voicemail to Kate, and a call from the residence in which Margaret had introduced herself by her maiden name and asked to speak to her own husband, who had been dead since

2009. The director had handled it. What Joanne wanted to know on the phone now, without saying so directly, was how many reds it was going to take.

Silence on the line. Through the south window the long shadow of the meadow was lengthening across what had been the kitchen garden. Outside, in the gravel lot, Ray's truck was idling. He had started it, but was still standing beside it, finishing his cigarette. The tip glowed and died, glowed and died.

"I'll call her in the morning," Kate said. "Nine thirty. She'll be more present at nine thirty."

"That's not what I'm asking."

"I know it's not."

"You're three states away."

"I know I'm three states away."

"For two weeks."

"For fourteen days."

"Kate."

"Joanne. The contract pays six months of wages. The contract is fourteen days, October twenty-eighth to November tenth. I can't get it from anywhere else."

Joanne did not answer immediately. Joanne was a hospital administrator. The math was the math. Joanne would not pretend otherwise.

"Fine. Call her in the morning. And call me Sunday."

"I'll call you Sunday."

"Kate."

"Yeah."

"She left you a long message."

"I listened to it."

"It's bad, isn't it."

"It's not good."

"Yeah."

A softer silence between them. Then Joanne said, "I love you," which she said sometimes when she was angry and sometimes when she was not, and Kate said "I love you too," which she said in approximately the same proportions, and they hung up.

Kate sat at the table.

The light through the south window was the last useful daylight. Her watch said five twelve. The contract said dawn to dark. There was still work to do.

She squared the blueprints and brought up the laptop's drafting program. She laid the 1873 originals down first, beside the 1923 reconstruction set, beside the 1947 expansion plan, in the order an architect reads them, which was the order they had been drawn.

She started with the central administration. The administration was always the part of an institutional building that lied least. Administration buildings had to function as administration, and architects of the period drew them the way they were going to be built, because the head of the institution was going to walk through them daily.

She moved out to the wings. The west wing's 1873 original plan and the 1947 expansion plan agreed on the west wing in every detail she could verify by eye against what she had walked through that afternoon, allowing for a stair the 1947 plan had moved by six feet. A normal renovation.

She turned to the east wing.

The east wing's 1923 reconstruction plan and the 1947 expansion plan disagreed.

She held them side by side under the lamp and traced the disagreement with the tip of her drafting pencil. The 1923 reconstruction set, drawn after the women's-wing demolition and rebuild, showed a service stair off the second-floor west corridor between Ward 2-E and the central staff station. It was six steps up to a half-landing, then six steps up to the third floor. A pair of double doors on the half-landing opened onto a closet for linens. The 1947 expansion plan did not show the stairs. The 1947 plan showed, in the same location, a wall.

She sat back. Took her glasses off. Set them on the table. Rubbed the bridge of her nose.

There were ordinary explanations. Building plans omitted things. Renovations between 1923 and 1947 could have removed the stairs. The 1947 draftsman could have been working from an incomplete reference set. None of this was necessarily a discrepancy in the building. It was, on the face of it, a discrepancy on the paper.

She put the glasses back on. Made a note in her field notebook:

East wing 2nd fl. service stair, west corridor, midpoint. On 1923 plan; not on 1947. Verify in person AM.

She closed the notebook.

Six oh two.

The south window had gone dark. The meadow was no longer visible. Inside the room the only light was the laptop's screen and the fluorescent panel overhead, which was also the only light she had wanted, since she would do another walk through of the building before she left for the night.

She did a shorter walk than the afternoon one. The afternoon walk had been the introduction. The evening walk was the closing-up. She moved through the ground floor with the headlamp on the low setting, checking what should not be on, what should not be open, what bag of hers might be where she had not meant to leave it. She found nothing she had not expected to find. Walked to the rear corridor that ran east toward the east wing. Walked the long corridor that went from the rear of the central administration past the chapel-corridor and out toward the chapel, which was detached, fifty yards behind the central building. She did not enter the chapel.

Instead, she walked the chapel-corridor.

It had not been on the 1873 plan. It had been added in the 1947 expansion. It was a connecting corridor between the central administration and the detached chapel, eighty feet long, brick on brick, three steps down at the chapel end because the chapel sat on lower ground. She had not, that afternoon, gone past the inner door at the administration end. She had marked it for the morning. She was there now only because it was on the way back to the foyer.

The temperature in the chapel-corridor was lower than the temperature in the corridor she had just stepped out of.

The thermometer on her tablet gave her a number for each. The corridor she had stepped out of: sixty-one degrees. The chapel-corridor: forty-six.

She stopped.

Stood in the doorway. Held the tablet up.

The reading held at forty-six for the count of thirty seconds.

She stepped into the chapel-corridor itself and walked five paces in. The reading held at forty-six.

She walked back into the rear corridor. Within four paces the reading climbed to fifty-eight. Then sixty. Then sixty-one.

A fifteen-degree differential. Sustained.

She stood in the rear corridor with the tablet in her hand and thought about it. She contemplated every anomaly she had ever logged in this work, which was to think first about masonry, then HVAC, then wiring, then animals, then, last and rarely, anything else. The chapel-corridor was an exterior-facing brick-on-brick passage with a slate roof in poor condition and three steps down at one end onto a chapel floor below grade. There was not, in any reasonable architectural read, a reason for it to be fifteen degrees colder than the interior corridor it adjoined. Five would have been ordinary. Eight would have been unusual but explicable. Fifteen was a number she would expect in a corridor with broken windows in the wind. There was no wind, and the windows in the chapel-corridor were shuttered.

She made a note:

Chapel-corridor: minus 15 F differential, sustained over 30s. 61 degrees in hall, 46 in corridor. Verify AM. Possible: roof failure, masonry void, ductwork. No wind tonight; windows shuttered.

She walked back to the foyer. Put on her jacket with the vest still on medium under it. The blanket she folded back over the chair for the morning. She turned off the laptop. Turned off the headlamp. Stood for a moment at the foot of the 1873 staircase and listened to the building settle into full dark.

The building settled. It said nothing it had not been saying since 1873. The radiators snapped twice. A floorboard above the foyer settled with the small ticking sound dry oak made when its day's breathing was over. The wind across the meadow, which had come up while she was inside, found its way into the chapel and made a sound that, to a person standing in the foyer of the central administration, would have sounded, for the half-second it took her to identify the source, like a human breath drawn slowly in.

She identified the source. Noted:

Wind in chapel; probable intake at the rear sash where the muntin is failing.

She let herself out through the front door, locked it, and walked to the car across the gravel.

The headlights came on. The dashboard glowed: clock, fuel gauge, the field thermometer she kept clipped to the air vent. Outside reading thirty-eight. Inside reading fifty-eight. She sat in the driver's seat with the engine running and the heat on low and for the count of a slow ninety seconds did not put the car in gear. The motel was forty-one miles south, at the far edge of the next county, on a county road off the state highway. She had reserved a room with two queens and a kitchenette. It was the kind of place that left a Bible in the drawer and a plug-in pine-scented thing in the bathroom that would leave a smell on her clothes for a week after she checked out.

She put the car in gear.

Drove down the access road at the speed limit.

In the rearview, Marston Hill stood the way it had stood since 1873. Central administration intact. West wing decaying ordinarily. East wing reconstructed once, in 1923, in a way the 1947 plan did not entirely account for. The bars on the upper-floor windows of the east wing were dark against the afterlight. The chapel-corridor between the administration and the detached chapel held its forty-six degrees.

Behind the second-floor wall of the east wing, between Ward 2-E and the central staff station, the closed throat of a service stair the 1947 plan had not bothered to draw held its 1923 brick, its 1923 mortar, and the 1923 dust nobody had moved in a hundred and three years.

Forty-one miles south. She drove past the foundation outline of a Mobil station that had closed in 2018. Past a horse field with two horses and a third that was either grazing or gone. Past the gate of a state park that had its sign down for the season. Past the welcome marker for the next county and the dark windows of a diner that had once been a Friendly's and was now an LLC operating under a name in a font nobody had bought since 1991.

The motel's vacancy sign was the orange of a forgotten porch light. The woman at the front desk had a paperback by her elbow and a hot-water cup the size of a child's shoe. Room 14, ground floor, parking out front. She slid the key across the laminate. It was a plastic fob, the kind motels still used because the chain hotels had not yet chosen to buy them.

Kate carried her field bag and the laptop case down the breezeway. Room 14 had the two queens, a kitchenette, and a thermostat set to seventy-five because the front-desk woman had let herself in earlier and turned it up. Kate set the field bag at the foot of the nearer bed. The other bed she would not use. She set the laptop on the kitchenette table, plugged it in, and opened it although she did not open the photogrammetry program yet.

She sat on the edge of the bed.

She did not call her mother or her sister. She did not call the editor at the preservation journal who had been waiting on a query letter for nine months. She sat on the edge of the bed and looked at the closed door of Room 14 and listened to the heater in the wall come on and go off and come on again on a cycle whose period she would learn by morning. The forecast said nor'easter on Wednesday. The watch on her wrist said nine thirty-eight. She was too tired to keep working. The note in her field notebook for tomorrow said: *chapel-corridor, service stair, Eleanor Ross.*

She set the watch alarm for five thirty.

ARCHIVE EXCERPT

Marston Hill State Hospital · Patient Admission Record · March 14, 1924

MARSTON HILL

PATIENT ADMISSION

DATE: March 14 1924

PATIENT: PEMBERTON Alice Margaret

AGE: 21

SEX: F

COMMITTED BY: husband (Pemberton, Charles W)

DIAGNOSIS ON ADMISSION: moral insanity hysteric tendencies, refusal of conjugal duties

EDUCATION: excessive (Bryn Mawr two years)

ADMITTED TO: East Wing Ward 2E

Patient is articulate, likely difficult

CHAPTER THREE

The survey begins

Day 2

'What crime was this, that lived incarnate in this sequestered mansion, and could neither be expelled nor subdued by the owner?"
— Charlotte Brontë, Jane Eyre (1847)

The fog came down off the hills at four in the morning and was still there when she pulled in at six twelve. The building did not come at her through the trees so much as appear: gray on gray, three meters from the chain-link before the chain-link itself was visible.

Ray had unlocked the gate already. The double-wide had a kitchen light on and a thread of woodstove smoke going straight up into a sky that was not moving. He was on the trailer step with a thermos and two enamel cups beside him, and he poured her one without asking.

"You drink it black."

"I drink it black."

"Sugar's inside if you change your mind."

"Black is fine."

She took the cup and stood beside him. They looked at the building together in the fog. It was the kind of looking trade people did at each other's projects, an interrogation through the corner of the eye.

"You sleep alright?"

"Six hours."

"At the Cedarwood."

"Off Route 8, yeah."

"Lori still at the desk?"

"With a paperback the size of a brick."

"That's Lori."

The coffee was strong and a little bitter the way coffee from a cheap thermos got after the second hour, which was right, because Ray would have made it at four thirty.

She suspected the fog was the kind that did not lift on its own; it would burn off when the sun cleared the ridge. She drank the coffee. He poured her another and she let him.

"The walk-through," she said.

"East first."

"East first."

"You want me on the cut team this morning, or with you."

"With me."

He opened the front door of the central administration with the same key from the same ring on the same belt loop and stood aside again. The building was its own temperature this morning, fifty-six degrees by her tablet. It was the cold that had made peace with the exterior overnight and not yet recovered from the predawn. She turned the heated vest up to high.

The breakers for the east wing were in the central stair landing, a row of fuses brought up to code in the eighties and failing since. Ray flipped them in order. The corridor lights on the lower floor came on with the slow yellow recovery of fluorescent tubes that had not been switched on in three years. The light was bad in the way fluorescents always were after long disuse. Half the tubes were flickering and two of them weren't lighting at all. Kate accepted this and did not flag it. The wreckers were going to cut power on the eighth.

"Stair," Ray said.

"Stair."

The central stair to the second floor was 1923 reform-era construction, oak treads with brass nosings, the brass worn smooth where it was worn at all and untouched in the corners where it had not been used since closure. She put a gloved hand on the banister at the landing and looked up the second flight before she went.

The second floor of the east wing was the women's ward. It had been the women's ward since 1873, and from the 1923 rebuild through the day in 1994 when the last patient was discharged or transferred or marked as transferred but possibly worse. The corridor was covered in linoleum the color of a tooth. It dropped at one end onto plywood the maintenance crew had laid in the eighties when the linoleum finally gave out. The doors of the patient rooms were six-paneled wood with viewing slots at adult eye level. The slots were covered with metal flaps on hinges which opened only from the corridor side. The doors also closed only from the corridor side.

She went down the corridor at her own pace and Ray let her. Ray had been in this corridor before. Demolition foreman on his second asylum could read the difference at a glance between a women's ward and a men's ward, and the difference lived in the doors and the size of the rooms and the placement of the viewing slots. He had nothing to add that she did not already know.

She stopped in front of the door to Ward 2-E and went in.

Ward 2-E was eight feet by ten. There was one window on the east elevation, barred. The bed had gone in '94. The radiator under the window was an original 1923 cast-iron unit, painted twice, the second time more recently. There was wear in the linoleum near the door at adult standing height and wear near the window at sitting height and a third pattern she had to look at twice before she identified it: a long oval of polished linoleum at the foot of where the bed had been. It was the kind of wear a person made with their feet over many years sitting on the edge of a mattress and not getting up.

She stood silent in Ward 2-E for the count of thirty.

Ray, in the corridor, did not come in.

She came out.

"East wing's got the seam," she said. "I want to find the stair."

"The one not on the '47."

"The one not on the '47."

She went back to the central staff station, pulled the 1923 plan from her field bag, laid it flat against the corridor wall with the legend up. The 1923 stair was supposed to be located fifteen feet east of the central staff station, in the wall between Ward 2-E and Ward 2-F. She paced it. Stopped at the wall fifteen feet east of the staff station. First, she put her ear to it, then her palm. The wall was 1923 brick on the inside face, plaster on top, and the plaster was old. Forty years old, maybe sixty.

Underneath, when she rapped with her knuckle, the wall sounded different from the wall on either side of it. The walls on either side gave back the dense, dry sound of brick on brick. The wall in front of her gave back a hollow sound.

She moved her knuckle three feet to the left and rapped. Brick. Three feet to the right. Brick. Came back to the eight-foot section in the middle. Hollow.

"Yeah," Ray said behind her. He had been there for a while.

"Yeah."

"Tape it."

She unclipped a roll of blue masking tape from the carabiner and ran a strip along the floor at the base of the hollow section. Then a second strip up the wall on the left side. Then a third up the wall on the right. Then a fourth across the top, eight feet up, on tiptoe. The blue tape on plaster was a rectangle eight feet wide and eight feet tall. The shape of a stairway.

"You want it on the cut order?" Ray said.

"Not yet. The wreckers can take this one in sequence. It comes down in the natural pull on November tenth."

"You want it noted."

"I want it noted. Photographed. And cross-referenced against the '23 plan in case I missed anything else."

She raised the Pentax and took a wide angle shot of the taped rectangle, two mediums, three close on the seams of the tape against plaster, and one of the corner where the brick was visible through a chip in the plaster face. She lowered the camera and made a note in her field notebook:

East wing 2nd fl., 15 ft E of central staff station, btw Ward 2-E and Ward 2-F: hollow space, ~8x8 ft, plaster intact. 1923 service stair sealed at landing, plastered over. NOT *on 1947 plan. Mark for natural-sequence pull on day 14.*

She closed the notebook.

The hydrotherapy basement was at the south end of the east wing, one flight down from the ground floor. The door was steel, painted the same institutional green as the file cabinets in the records room, deadbolted with a Mosler five-pin gone the color of old pennies at the keyway. It was the kind of lock that took a key Eleanor Ross had not been required to return in 1994 because Eleanor Ross had not been asked. The kind of lock you could pick if you had to. Kate did not try to pick it.

Ray stood beside her and looked at the door.

"Five and a half hours to get a locksmith out from the regional office," he said. "If we put in a request."

"I'll set up an interview with Eleanor instead, through her granddaughter. The registry has the granddaughter as the contact line."

"The granddaughter."

"Tessa. Nursing student."

"She'll let her grandmother give you a key to the basement of an asylum?"

"She'll let her grandmother give me an interview. After the interview has progressed far enough, if her grandmother trusts me, the key may come up. Or it may not."

"Or it may not."

"I can wait. Eleanor isn't going anywhere this week and the basement isn't either."

Ray looked at her, and looked at the door, and looked at her again.

"You're patient, Welton."

"Patient is the only thing the work allows for."

By eleven thirty they had walked the rest of the east wing's second floor and most of the third. The third floor was the worst preserved of the floors. It was the section the wreckers were going to pull first, which was fine, because the third told her the same story the second told her, only louder, and she had already taken the second's picture.

They came down the central stair. Ray's radio went off at the ground-floor landing.

"Gate," they heard. "Got a guy."

He pressed talk. "Yeah."

"Says he's a doctor in town. His father used to run the place. Wants to introduce himself."

Kate, two steps below Ray, stopped on the stair.

"Wendell Kessler."

Ray looked at her. "You know him?"

"I know of him. Call sheet."

"He's on the call sheet?"

"Sort of. His father is. The father's dead. The son's a courtesy line. Send him up."

Ray pressed talk. "Send him to the trailer. We'll come down."

Wendell Kessler was waiting at the trailer step. He was fifty-seven, which she knew from the call sheet. He was wearing the kind of barn coat a local doctor wore on a Thursday morning that he had cleared from his calendar so he could pretend he had been driving by. He had a thermos of his own, a stainless Stanley with a worn blue grip. He stood up from the step when he saw them coming.

"Welton," he said, smiling. "Kate. Wendell Kessler."

He used her first name on the first sentence. She noticed it.

"Dr. Kessler."

"Wendell, please. I won't keep you long. I should have called ahead. I was on my way to the office and couldn't quite let myself drive past."

"Your office is in town?"

"On Howard Street. The other side of the rotary."

"Six miles."

"More like seven by the road. I came through the meadow side."

He smiled again. His smile was easy and warm but offered nothing. It was the smile of a man who had practiced his smile in front of a mirror at twenty-two and had not changed it since.

"My father was the medical director here," he said. "From '72 to closure. Theo Kessler. I grew up on the grounds. The director's house was at the back of the cemetery property. The state sold it off in '96. I interned here in '88 and '89. I went into private practice in town after closure. I'm on the medical board, the historical society board, and I'm treasurer at the Rotary. I'm not stopping by because I want anything from you. I thought I could help."

Kate let the speech finish. He had given it before, perhaps to himself in the car on the drive in. The sentences had been smoothed.

"Welcome," she said.

"Thank you. May I walk..."

"To the trailer. Yes. The building's a hard hat zone, as you know."

"Ah, yes."

He glanced at the building over her shoulder. The fog had burned off, finally, and the east wing was visible at full morning, the bars dark on the upper floors, the seam between '73 and '23 a vertical line in two colors of brick. He looked at the bars half a second longer than was casual.

"I haven't been on the property for three years," he said.

"They take a while to come back to."

"They do."

A short pause. He took a sip of his thermos. She took out the field notebook, opened it to a blank page, set it on the trailer step, and sat down beside Ray's empty cup.

"Dr. Kessler. What can I do for you?"

"Wendell."

"What can I do for you?"

He smiled a third time and did not answer for a beat. The smile was now a slightly different smile, and his eyes were no longer trying to be easy.

"Are you alone here at night?" he said.

She gave herself the second she needed before she answered.

"I'm not on-site overnight."

"Of course. But once you've left for the day. Are you alone where you're staying?"

"No."

He looked at her and did not press. He noted the answer in some private way that was not hidden from her. He tipped the thermos.

"I asked because the building draws kids," he said. "Local kids find these places. The state should put a guard on the gate. I'm going to write the state about it."

"Please do."

"Anyway. I won't keep you. If I can be helpful with anything, my father kept patient records at the house. I've got boxes. Let me know."

"Thank you."

"I mean it."

"Sounds like it."

He stood up. He had one more line. He had been holding it for the last sentence.

"It's good," he said. "What you're doing here. I want you to know that. It's important."

She did not reply to this. The reply he wanted would have been a thank you. The reply she gave him was a nod that took a long second to arrive and was not warm. He noticed it.

Ray, beside her, did not turn his head as the car backed out of the gravel lot and turned onto the access road. The car went three hundred yards and disappeared into the trees.

Ray did not turn his head. "How alone are you, Welton."

"Pretty alone, Mendez."

"Yeah."

"Yeah."

She went back into the building. The afternoon was for the rest of the third floor and for cross-checking the 1923 plan against everything she had taped that morning. She had four hours of light. She made another note in the field notebook on the page below the stair note:

W. Kessler on-site 11:50, departed 12:08. Cleared own calendar. Stated motive: family interest. Used first name without invitation. Asked re: nighttime occupancy and where I sleep. Note: knows the layout. Note: said he hasn't been on property in three years. Note: he has been on property more recently than that.

She closed the notebook. She went back to the east wing where she got more light.

CHAPTER FOUR

A wing that should not be there

Day 3

"Something there is that doesn't love a wall."
— Robert Frost, "Mending Wall" (1914)

She was at the gate at six twenty-six. Ray had unlocked it already and was at the trailer with his thermos and a second cup poured. She raised her cup as she went past, and he raised his, and they did not need to say anything else. The IR survey was the part of the day that would not wait.

The infrared camera was a FLIR T-Series she had been carrying since her second contract. She trusted it the way she trusted a level. Within the conditions of its calibration, it could not lie. Read carefully, it would show you the inside of a wall.

She had it on the tripod by the central staff station of the east wing's second floor at six twenty-eight, civil twilight plus eight, with the corridor lights on and the temperature differential between the corridor (sixty-two) and the patient rooms (fifty-eight) sufficient for the camera to read the partitions cleanly. The IR survey was part of the work she liked best. It was the part the building hated.

She started at the south end of the corridor and moved north. Each patient room, she swept the camera across the four walls in a slow horizontal pan, then a slow vertical, then a diagonal. The walls of the east wing were 1923 brick on the inside face, plastered with two coats of lime over horsehair, the partitions between rooms framed with dimensioned lumber and lath that had gone half to dust by 1995 and was, by 2026, no longer doing structural work in any meaningful sense. The IR camera read warm where the brick was warmest and cool where the air had pooled in the cavities, and the difference in the patient rooms was usually three degrees. It was the difference of an ordinary cavity wall containing nothing but lath, plaster dust, and the residue of three quarters of a century of mice.

She came to Ward 2-E at seven oh three.

The wall she had taped the day before was on the north side of 2-E, between 2-E and 2-F, the side hiding the 1923 service staircase. She did not need the camera there. She had already read the stair with her knuckles. She moved the camera onto the south wall of 2-E instead, the partition shared with Ward 2-D, and ran a slow horizontal pan.

The screen of the FLIR went dark.

Not slightly cool. Dark. Fifteen-degree differential. A void the size of a closet. Or a chamber.

She held the camera steady, took a still, then another. She panned vertical. The dark void ran from the floor to a height of approximately seven feet. She panned horizontal again. The dark void ran approximately eight feet along the wall.

She lowered the camera.

She crossed the corridor and went into Ward 2-D. The room was a mirror of 2-E, eight by ten, single barred window on the east elevation, radiator under the window. She set up the tripod. Ran a horizontal pan across the south wall of 2-D, the partition shared with

2-C. She noted the three-degree differential. Ordinary cavity. She moved the tripod to the north wall, the partition shared with 2-E. Ran the pan.

The screen went dark in the same place. Eight feet wide. Floor to seven feet up.

A void between 2-D and 2-E. Visible from both sides and not found on either blueprint set.

She sat down on the radiator under the window and looked at the screen. The vest under her jacket was on medium and the radiator was cold so she did not stay long.

There was an architectural reading in which a void between two patient rooms of the dimensions she was seeing, was a chase for plumbing or electrical. There was another reading in which it was a closet for linens that had been sealed off and forgotten. There was a third in which it was a service space for the staff to move between corridors without entering the rooms. None of these were indicated on the 1923 plan. Nor the 1947 plan. They both showed Ward 2-E and Ward 2-D as adjacent rooms sharing a single partition wall sixteen inches thick.

What the IR was showing her was a cavity inside that partition.

A cavity inside a sixteen-inch partition would be eight inches deep, maximum, with eight inches of brick on each face, sufficient for plumbing and wiring and a service space at a stretch. It was not sufficient for the dimensions she was reading on the camera, which was reading a void seven feet high and eight feet long. A void seven feet high meant a partition wall twice the thickness of the one shown on the plans.

The plans were wrong. Or the wall was wrong. Or both.

She got up and moved the tripod back into 2-E. She took a final still then made the note:

East wing 2nd fl., btw Ward 2-D and Ward 2-E: thermal void, ~8 ft long x 7 ft high, fifteen-degree differential. Partition wall thickness on plans: 16 in. Wall thickness in fact: minimum 32 in (probably more). Void on neither 1923 nor 1947 plan. Mark for cut order, day 8.

She closed the notebook. Carried the camera in its case down to the trailer.

Ray was at the trailer with a clipboard. The cut crew was scheduled to begin first cuts on Day 8, exterior breaches in the west wing for asbestos remediation, and the cut order was a state-mandated protocol that documented what was going to be opened, in what sequence, by whom. Kate could write a cut order for a specific feature without filing an amendment. She did this routinely. She did not need permission. She needed to write the order clearly enough that the cut foreman, who would not be Ray, would do exactly what she told him to do and not a millimeter more.

She wrote the order. East wing, second floor, partition between 2-D and 2-E, central section, eight feet wide, seven feet high. Open at center with a four-inch pilot core. Stop. Hold for survey supervisor.

Ray read it.

"Eight on the eighth."

"Eight on the eighth."

"Day 8 is Wednesday."

"Day 8 is Wednesday."

"You want the union saw or my saw."

"Your saw."

"Yeah."

He took the order. Stamped it. Filed it.

It was twelve forty when the phone rang in her pocket. She was eating a sandwich on the trailer step, a turkey on a kaiser she had picked up at the Cedarwood's vending machine that morning. It was the kind of sandwich that came in a clamshell and did not promise anything. She took the phone out.

Mom.

She looked at the screen. Two rings. Three. On the fourth she answered.

"Hi, Mom."

"Kate. Sweetheart."

The voice was Margaret's, the way she had been in 2018, which was the year Kate had stopped expecting it. The librarian's careful rhythm. The slight dryness at the end of each sentence that was Margaret laughing at herself in a way nobody else heard.

"Are you well."

"I'm well. I'm at work."

"At... Joanne told me at the asylum. The contract."

"At Marston Hill, yes."

"How does it look."

"It looks like a Kirkbride that was rebuilt in 1923 and is going to come down on November tenth. It's a building, Mom."

"Oh, Kate."

A pause. Margaret did not fill pauses on her good hours. Margaret had spent twenty years as a high-school librarian and knew that a pause was a thing you let a young person sit in until they decided what they wanted to say.

"I called you yesterday," Margaret said. "I've been told. I don't remember calling you. I don't remember the message. Joanne played it for me this morning. I'm sorry, sweetheart."

"Mom. There's nothing to apologize for."

"There is. I left you a long message, and I wasn't myself. Will you come visit? After this."

"After the contract."

"After the contract."

"I'll come on the eleventh of November."

"The eleventh."

"The contract ends on the tenth, plus a day for travel. I'll be there."

A pause again. Margaret was thinking, on her good hour, about what she was going to forget tomorrow. Kate was thinking about the same thing.

"Tell me about the building."

"Mom."

"Tell me. I want to think about it."

"It's a Kirkbride. The wings angle away from the central administration. There is original 1873 brick on the men's side. The women's side was rebuilt in 1923 and the seam between the two clays is visible at fifty yards. The chapel is detached. The chapel-corridor is colder than the rest of the building, for a reason I can't explain. There are bars on the upper-floor windows of the women's wing that have never been removed. The lock on the hydrotherapy basement is a Mosler five-pin and the only key is held by the head nurse who retired in '94."

"Mosler."

"You remember Moslers."

"I remember the one on the back door of the high-school storeroom. It would not turn on humid days. Dad replaced it in '78."

"Dad replaced everything in '78."

"He did."

"I'm setting up an interview with the head nurse this week."

"What's her name."

"Eleanor Ross."

"Eleanor."

"Mm."

"I knew an Eleanor at the library. She read every Updike."

"This Eleanor is going to be eighty-two next year."

"Bring her flowers."

"Mom."

"Yellow."

"Yellow flowers?"

"For an old nurse, yellow."

"I'll bring her yellow flowers, Mom."

"Good."

"I love you."

"I love you too, sweetheart. Come on the eleventh."

"On the eleventh."

She hung up.

She sat on the trailer step with the phone in her hand and the half-eaten kaiser on her knee and looked at the building. The fog had been gone for hours. The east wing was visible in full October light. The bars on the upper floors were dark against pale brick.

Ray, inside the trailer, did not come out. He had heard the call through the open door. He was the kind of man who knew the difference between a call that needed company and a call that didn't need to be witnessed.

The kaiser had gone cold on her knee. The mayonnaise had begun to seep through the bottom slice. She put what was left of it in the trailer's trash on her way back to the building. The next thing on her list was the third floor.

She went back into the building. There was an afternoon of work and she had an afternoon's light to do it in. She finished the IR survey of the second floor and went up to the third. The third floor's partitions read clean. Three-degree differential everywhere. Ordinary cavity. Lath and plaster and dust. She moved the tripod through every patient room and every staff alcove and every bathroom on the third floor and the camera read the same dull confirmatory three degrees in every one of them.

By six the corridor lights had come on against the early dusk and the third floor was done.

She came back down to the second. Took down the tripod. Packed the camera in its case.

She walked the corridor of the second floor one more time before she left, as a way of saying to it: I've seen what I came to see today, I'll be back tomorrow. This was a habit. She had stopped explaining it to herself.

The corridor was its own dusk by the time she walked it. The fluorescents had gone yellow on the second pass. The plywood at the end of the linoleum was a paler color in the bad light. The window at the south end of the corridor admitted a long bar of horizontal sunlight that fell across the floorboards and lit the wear pattern outside the door of Ward 2-E. Then it went.

At the end of the corridor she stopped.

A sound.

She held still. Held the camera case at her side. Listened.

The sound was faint. It was wet and rhythmic. It seemed to be coming from behind the plaster.

It was three feet from her left shoulder. The wall there was the partition between Ward 2-E and Ward 2-D. The wall hiding the void she had marked that morning.

She listened.

The sound came in a slow regular interval, the interval of a slow breath. The sound was wet the way a thing in water moved. It was behind plaster, and Kate was a preservation architect and there were ordinary explanations for sounds behind plaster in a hundred-and-fifty-three-year-old building whose pipes had been switched off in 2022 and not refilled and not bled and not pressurized. She ran through the reasons.

Pipes. Settling pipes were the obvious read. Pipes had been off since 2022, dry on the lines, but a partly-flooded riser in a cavity could still be slowly losing pressure into something. This reason was possible. Not satisfying.

Animal. A nesting cat, a colony of something. Animals in cavity walls did not pulse on regular intervals as a rule. Animals were arrhythmic. They were either still or thrashing. She deemed this reason unlikely.

Ductwork. The HVAC had been off since 2022. Air would not be moving. She mentally shelved this one.

Settling masonry. A slow rhythmic sound from settling masonry was not a thing she had encountered in twenty years of work with buildings.

She listened another fifteen seconds.

The sound continued.

She took the field notebook out of her side pocket. Opened it to the page below the IR note. Wrote:

East wing 2nd fl. corridor, ~3 ft S of doorway to Ward 2-E: faint sound behind plaster, wet, rhythmic, slow interval (~1 sec). Heard at 18:11. Sustained at least 30 s. Possible: pipes settling (off since 2022), animal in cavity, ductwork (off), masonry settling. Pipes most plausible. Verify AM.

She underlined the last sentence. Closed the notebook.

She walked the rest of the corridor at her own pace. She did not run. She did not walk fast. She walked in the same measured way a level walked across a floor, deliberately focusing on her measured steps.

She locked the front door behind her at six twenty-four. Stood on the portico for the count of ten and looked at the meadow. The wind across the meadow had not come up. There was a light on in the trailer. Ray was inside, finishing his end-of-day paperwork.

She got into the Outback.

The dashboard glowed. Outside reading thirty-six. Inside reading sixty-two. The note in her field notebook for tomorrow said: *third floor west wing IR, chapel-corridor temp re-check; Eleanor through Tessa, verify wall sound.*

Forty-one miles to the Cedarwood.

She drove south.

CHAPTER FIVE

The first body

Day 4

"What, excepting torture, would produce insanity quicker than this treatment?"
— Nellie Bly, Ten Days in a Mad-House (1887)

She was at Ward 2-E at six twenty-eight with the field notebook open. She heard nothing.

The corridor was the same as the day before, only slightly drier in its acoustic, the way buildings were always slightly drier in their acoustic at six in the morning than at six in the evening because the temperature had not yet had the day to flex the joints. The fluorescents had not been turned on. She had the headlamp on instead, set to red because red was less likely to startle whatever in the wall might or might not still be there.

She listened for about a minute.

The wall did not pulse. The wall did not breathe. The wall was just as silent as it should be at six in the morning on a Saturday that was forecast to be the last clear morning before the storm.

She wrote in the notebook:

East wing 2nd fl. corridor, 06:28: no recurrence of sound from 18:11 prior. Wall silent, sustained 60 s. Indeterminate.

She closed the notebook.

If there had been a witness in the wall, the witness had withdrawn. There was no one to corroborate. She was not, professionally, a person who needed corroboration to log what she had logged the day before. However, she was a person who needed it to dismiss the log. She did not dismiss the log. She went down to the trailer.

Ray was on the trailer step. The fog this morning was thinner than the fog yesterday, with a wind coming off the meadow that put it in motion. He had the thermos and the second cup.

"Wall."

"Silent."

"Yeah."

He poured. She drank.

"Chapel-corridor next."

"Chapel-corridor, then west wing basement. I want to look at the morgue."

"The west wing morgue."

"Roof gave way in '96. The duct work in there should be reading air now, with the storm coming."

"You want me on the bore."

"Yes. Bring the borescope. The eight-millimeter."

"Yeah."

She measured the chapel-corridor at seven oh two. The reading was forty-six. The reading from the corridor she had stepped out of was sixty-one. She did not stay long. The chapel-corridor on Day 4 was the same chapel-corridor she had observed on Days 1 to 3, sustaining its forty-six degrees against everything, and she filed the new reading in the existing entry and went on.

She did not go into the chapel. She had not, on any of the days, gone into the chapel. The chapel was on the schedule for Day 6. The chapel was a thing you worked up to which she had learned from her previous closures.

Ray had the bore kit on his shoulder when she came out of the rear corridor.

"West."

"West."

They went to the west wing through the connecting corridor on the ground floor, passing the central staff station of the men's wing, which had been a staff station from 1873 through closure and which was, at this date, an empty alcove with a writing desk against one wall and the four nail holes where a clock had hung above it. The men's wing on the ground floor was its own ordinary closure-eve mess: paint failing on the corridor walls, the linoleum underfoot of the same wear pattern as the women's-wing linoleum but unmarked by a 1923 reform-era reconstruction, cracks where cracks had been since the '96 storm. She did not stop. Ray did not stop.

The west wing's basement was at the south end, accessed through a heavy hatch door with a hinge on the right side that had failed sometime in the eighties and been replaced with a plain steel pintle and gudgeon. Ray pushed it open. The smell on the staircase down was wet plaster and rat and the fungal note of any basement that had had a partial roof failure thirty years ago and been left to its own equilibrium. Kate's tablet thermometer read fifty-three.

The morgue was at the south end of the basement, behind a doorway whose door had been removed in '96 and not replaced. There were two slabs of porcelain, one full and one half collapsed into the floor where the joists below had given. She noted a drain in the center floor with a brass cap on it. The walls were painted the same institutional green as the records-room cabinets, though the green had gone the color a lime-based green went after thirty years of basement, which was a color it would be a courtesy not to name. The overhead light was a single porcelain socket with no bulb in it. A wash basin in the corner had a tap on it that had been turned off at the riser in 1994. Ray's flashlight, on a tripod he had unfolded by the doorway, lit the room from the door inward at an angle that left the corners dark.

An overhead heat duct ran east to west across the ceiling, crimped at the east end where the roof failure had collapsed the joist above it, accessible at the west end through a register that had been removed for service in 1986 and never reinstalled.

Ray stood at the west register with the bore.

"You want me to go first."

"Yes."

He fed the borescope cable up into the duct. The screen on the bore was a four-inch LCD that had been bright in 2014 and was less bright in 2026, but bright enough. He fed the cable twelve inches at a time, advancing the camera in a slow corkscrew that would let it see all four faces of the duct's interior. The screen showed sheet metal. Sheet metal. Crimp. Sheet metal. Then a diagonal of something pale.

He stopped.

"Welton."

"Yeah."

"Look."

She came over and looked at the screen.

The pale diagonal on the screen was the proximal third of a human femur, lying lengthwise in the duct, its head against the crimp where the roof had collapsed the joist and its shaft running west toward the camera. The femur was the color of old ivory.

She did not say anything for the count of three.

"Femur."

"Femur," Ray said.

"Get a still."

He clicked the still, saved it, pulled the camera back six inches and took another. He pulled it back six inches more, took a third, then pulled the cable out.

She stepped back from the duct and took out the field notebook. She wrote:

West wing basement, old morgue, west register of E-W heat duct: human femur (apparent), proximal third visible, lying lengthwise approx. 18 in. inside duct from west register. Camera stills available. Discovery time: 11:07. Verified by R. Mendez.

She closed the notebook.

"Call the county," she said.

"Yeah."

He went up the stairs to call the county.

She sat on the floor of the morgue with her back to the porcelain slab and looked at the brass cap on the floor drain, which was the kind of brass cap that had been screwed into a floor in 1924 and had not been unscrewed since, and she let her mind be still for three minutes. This was a thing she had learned to do on her second contract, when the corner of a wall in a Vermont orphanage had given up a third bone. Three minutes. The body's clock, not hers.

After three minutes she stood up.

She stood up the way she always stood up after the three minutes, which was the way of a level returning to plumb, and she went to the west register and took out the bore one more time and ran the camera around the duct she had not yet examined and confirmed there was nothing else visible. She noted the absence. She went up the stairs.

Ray was at the trailer with his radio. He had called the county at eleven oh nine and the county had called him back at eleven fourteen. The state forensic anthropologist was already on a job in the next county over and would be on-site by two. He had not gotten her name.

He had told her there was a bone in a duct. She had said yes, she would come.

Kate sat on the trailer step and drank a third cup of Ray's coffee, which was now on the fourth hour, and the bitterness of it was the right bitterness for a Saturday on which the next thing to do was wait. She called the state forensic emergency line in the capital from the trailer's landline at eleven thirty-six, was patched through to the duty archivist, who was forty-something and tired and helpful. She agreed to set up an emergency request for the 1924 to 1940 admissions and discharge records pulled forward to her by Tuesday. She wrote down the duty archivist's name. Ray, beside her, finished a cigarette.

The hours between eleven thirty-six and one fifty-eight were the hours, on any job, that had to be sat through. Ray sat through them with her. He had a paperback in the trailer, the kind that lived on the trailer dashboard, but he did not get it.

Dr. Renata Owens arrived at one fifty-eight. The state forensic anthropologist drove a Subaru of her own, an older Forester, dark green, the back full of cases. She came down to the basement with Ray and a young assistant whose name Kate did not catch the first time and got the second. Owens was fifty-two, gray and very tall, in field clothes that had been field clothes for twenty years.

"Welton."

"Owens."

"Tell me about the bore."

Kate told her. Owens went to the duct, set up her own scope, and explored the duct in fifteen minutes the way Kate could read walls in fifteen. It was a foreman's read, fast and final. She extracted the femur with a long-handled grip and laid it on a sterile cloth on the partially-collapsed slab. She measured. She turned. She set the cloth open as Kate came over and stood at her shoulder.

"Late nineteenth or early twentieth," Owens said.

"How sure."

"On the femur alone, eighty percent. On the femur and the duct it was in, ninety-five."

"Why ninety-five."

"Because the duct is 1924 ductwork with mid-century retrofit. The femur went into that duct after 1924 and before the duct was retrofitted, which the screws in the register collar suggest was somewhere around 1947 or '52. Forty-year window. Late nineteenth or early twentieth pulled forward by five decades. Female, probably. Twenties to forties at death. Slightly malnourished. No tool marks."

"Closure-era irregular disposal."

"Closure of this institution was 1994. This is older than that. This is a pre-WWII irregular disposal. Asylum staff in the twenties and thirties did this when a patient died unclaimed and the cemetery ledger was full, or when paperwork was inconvenient. Not unprecedented."

"You've seen this before."

"Six asylums, three TB sanatoria, one prison. Yes."

"Records will be in the state archive."

"What survived of them. I'd start with the 1924 to 1940 admissions, cross-reference against discharges marked destination unrecorded."

"I've already requested it."

"Good. We'll take her in for full workup."

Owens packed the femur. The young assistant, whose name was Hector, took the camera stills off the bore. The whole interaction had taken under two hours. Owens stopped at the morgue door on her way out.

"Welton."

"Owens."

"This won't be the only one."

She went up the stairs. Hector followed.

Kate came up the stairs ten minutes after Owens did. The light at the top of the stairs was the sodium-color of an October afternoon at three.

Ray was at the trailer talking to a man in a barn coat who had a thermos. Wendell. He had clearly seen Owens's Forester pull out of the gate and come to be on-site afterward. He turned when Kate came across the gravel.

"Kate."

"Dr. Kessler."

"Wendell, please. Ray was telling me. May I say I'm so sorry."

"Why are you sorry."

He took half a step back, smiling.

"For what you found. For the paperwork it creates. I know the protocols."

"You know the protocols."

"My father ran them."

He let that sit. The smile was the same smile from yesterday. The eyes were not smiling at all.

"Listen," he said. "I want to be helpful. My father's records, the boxes I have at the house, are mostly closure-era, '85 forward. There is some older material. I have not catalogued it. If you want to come by, you can dig through whatever's there. I'll make space. I could have it on the dining room table in two hours."

"Thank you. That's generous."

"I mean it."

"I'll come back to you on it."

"Today?"

"Tomorrow at the earliest. I'm waiting on a state archive intake. They have the official surviving record, and I want to know what's in the official record before I look at what's in your dining room."

"Smart."

"Yes."

He looked at her. The smile thinned slightly, not in a way most people would have caught, but in a way she did.

"Tomorrow then."

"Maybe tomorrow. I'll let you know."

He tipped the thermos, said goodbye to Ray, and walked to his car. The car backed out of the gravel lot and turned onto the access road and disappeared into the trees.

Ray, beside her: "He came in twenty minutes after Owens left."

"He must have been close."

"Or he's been close most of the day."

"Yes."

Ray turned to the tree line. He kept his gaze there.

She wrote in the field notebook:

W. Kessler on-site 14:55, departed 15:21. Showed within 20 min of Owens departure. Offered access to father's records (boxes at his house). Offered to set the table within 2 hours. Note: too eager. Note: knew the closure-era protocols. Will request state archive intake first; will not visit Kessler house alone if I visit at all.

She closed the notebook.

The wreckers were due to start staging on the eighth. She had four working days before the building came down on her schedule, and one bone in a duct, and one void in a wall, and one stair that was supposed to be a closet, and one wet rhythmic sound the wall was no longer making, and an offer she did not intend to take from a man who had used her first name without invitation in their first conversation.

She had a list.

She had four hours of light.

The wreckers had been on a fourteen-day clock when she signed the contract. Since the femur, the clock had quietly become her clock. Ten days from a

Saturday afternoon in October to the morning the wreckers cut the East Wing into the bed of the first truck. She had a bone in a state lab, a void she had marked for cut, a sealed stair, a wet sound the wall had taken back, and now Wendell Kessler's dining room. Ten days, she thought, and went back to the building.

CHAPTER SIX

The storm

Day 5

"There are things in that paper which nobody knows but me, or ever will."
— Charlotte Perkins Gilman, The Yellow Wallpaper (1892)

The nor'easter came two days early.

She was driving in at six twenty in the predawn dark. The radio in the Outback had told her it was a cold front, gusts to fifty-five, intermittent rain through the morning, heavy rain by two, full storm conditions sustained through the night and into Tuesday. She had registered this on the drive.

She got to the gate at six twenty-six. Ray's truck was on the access road behind her ninety seconds later. He had been at home, not the trailer, which meant he had been on his roof, taping his own slate against the storm.

By eight in the morning the wind was howling through the meadow and by nine the rain had found the gaps in the chapel slate. At ten, the construction generator that had been lighting the upper floors of both wings was no longer able to light the upper floors of both wings. Ray took the cut crew off the third floor, took the sheeting crew off the west elevation, sent everyone but his own foreman home. Kate, on the radio at ten oh four, told him she would work in the records room.

"In the dark."
"By headlamp."
"Welton."
"Mendez."
"Fine."

The records room was at the south end of the rear corridor of the central administration. She had walked through it on Day 1, marked it for inventory on Day 2, set it aside for a slow afternoon. The slow afternoon had arrived. Her headlamp was on full. The administrator's office across the corridor had the camp chair and the lap blanket; she had brought both. The vest under her jacket was set to high.

The records room was twenty by twenty-four with a plaster ceiling, dropped acoustic tile fallen in two places, and file cabinets standing along all four walls. The cabinets were the kind the state had bought by the gross in the seventies, painted institutional green, drawers labeled in faded sharpie. The records had left in 1994 but the cabinets had stayed because the state did not pay to remove what nobody would buy.

By ten the wind off the meadow had come through at a sustained thirty-two miles per hour with gusts to forty-eight. The rear corridor and the foyer were dropping a degree an hour as the storm pulled the building's warmth out through the loose slate and the failing windows. The chapel-corridor, where Kate had stopped for a reading on her way past at nine forty, was at forty-six. It had been forty-six on Day 1. It had been forty-six this morning at six. It was at forty-six in a fifty-mile wind. The chapel-corridor was the only room in the central administration that was not paying attention to the storm. The records room was the warmest room only because it had no windows on an exterior wall.

The inventory was a dull job. She did it in pencil on a pad she carried for the purpose, drawer by drawer, top to bottom, left to right, in the order an architect observed a wall. She started at the cabinet nearest the door.

ADMISSIONS 1968 to 1972: empty.

ADMISSIONS 1973 to 1978: empty.

ADMISSIONS 1979 to 1984: empty.

ADMISSIONS 1985 to 1990: empty, with a single brass paperclip stuck to the bottom liner, which she did not remove.

ADMISSIONS 1991 to 1994: empty.

DISCHARGE 1968 to 1972: empty.

DISCHARGE 1973 to 1978: empty.

She moved to the next cabinet.

DISCHARGE 1923 to 1928.

She pulled the drawer. The drawer slid on its rollers the way drawers slid on rollers that had been replaced in the eighties and not opened since, with a small dry click and a slight resistance.

The drawer contained one sheet of paper.

She stood there with the headlamp on full and looked at the drawer for the count of five. Then she put on a pair of nitrile gloves from the box in her field bag. She lifted the sheet out of the drawer with the kind of two-handed care a preservation architect used on a 1924 paper that had survived a hundred and two years of an institutional file cabinet, and laid it on the top of the cabinet, and bent the headlamp at it.

The sheet was an intake form. It was in the wrong drawer. The drawer was discharge.

PATIENT ADMISSION RECORD
MARSTON HILL STATE HOSPITAL
DATE: March 14, 1924
Patient: PEMBERTON, Alice Margaret
Age: 21
Sex: F
Committed by: husband (Pemberton, Charles W.)
Diagnosis on admission: moral insanity, hysteric tendencies, refusal of conjugal duties
Education: excessive (Bryn Mawr, two years)
Admitted to: East Wing, Ward 2-E
Annotation in pencil, sideways, signed E.C.: Patient is articulate. Likely difficult.

She read the form twice. Then she stood there with her gloved hands at her sides and read it a third time with the headlamp turned three degrees to the right so she could see the pencil annotation more clearly, and did not move for the count of forty.

Ward 2-E. The room she had stood in on Day 2. The room across the wall from the void she had marked on Day 3. The room three feet north of where she had logged a wet rhythmic sound the wall had not made when she returned at six the next morning to verify it.

The annotation: E.C. The research she had done told her E.C. was Edmund Caldwell, the founding superintendent. Caldwell had retired in 1899 and died in 1908 by the surviving record. The 1924 annotation was therefore not in his hand. The annotation was in his initials.

The form said *patient is articulate. Likely difficult.* It said this in pencil, sideways, in handwriting that was old without being shaky, in initials that belonged to a man dead sixteen years by the time the form was filled out.

Caldwell's son had not gone into medicine. The state archive had no record of an E. Caldwell at the institution after 1908.

She raised the Pentax. She took eight stills of the form: a wide, two mediums, three close, one of the pencil annotation, and one of the date stamp at the top right where the institution had rubber-stamped the date in violet ink. She lowered the camera.

She took the SD card out of the Pentax and put it in the SD card reader on her laptop. The stills imported. She opened the third one, the close on the patient name, to verify it had captured the pencil work. It had.

She closed the laptop.

She did not put the form back in the drawer.

She left the form on the top of the cabinet, weighted with the SD card reader, and she went across the corridor to the administrator's office to write a notation on the inventory pad. The notation took her twenty seconds.

She went back across the corridor.

The form was gone.

The form was not on the cabinet. It was not on the floor. It was not in the drawer she had taken it from. It was not in any of the drawers immediately adjacent. It was not on the windowsill, on the radiator, behind the radiator, under the cabinet, or against the baseboard.

She got down on her hands and knees with the headlamp on full.

It was not under any cabinet. It was not behind any cabinet. It was not in any of the cabinets she had already inventoried. She went through every drawer in every cabinet in the records room she had already documented and she did not find it. She went into the administrator's office across the corridor and did not find it. She went into the foyer and did not find it. She came back to the records room and stood with the headlamp on the empty top of the cabinet where she had left it and did not find it.

She had photographed it.

The eight photographs were on the laptop.

The form itself was gone.

Kate, on her hands and knees in a closure-eve asylum during a nor'easter at twelve oh two on Day 5 of a fourteen-day contract, was a person of a methodical disposition who had searched a room twice and found nothing. The methodical disposition had a ceiling. She was at it now.

She got up off her hands and knees. She pulled the gloves off, balled them up and set them on top of the cabinet where the form had been. She put on a fresh pair. She went through the cabinets she had already inventoried a third time anyway, because going through the cabinets a third time was thorough.

The phone in her jacket pocket buzzed at twelve oh nine. She took it out.

Mom.

The screen rang for the count of seven and went to voicemail on eight.

She put the phone back in her pocket.

This was a not-lucid call. The lucid call had been Day 3. Today was the not-lucid Margaret, which meant the call was a Margaret she could not help. She would call Joanne tonight. The signal at Marston Hill in a nor'easter was inconsistent at best; she would call from the motel.

In the online journal Joanne kept and color-coded, the not-lucid Margaret was a yellow at the low end of yellow trending toward red. Today's call would be marked. Joanne would call her after the residence's evening meal and tell her in three sentences how the day had gone. Kate would not, tonight, tell Joanne about the form. There were forms of news Joanne could not take on the day a yellow trended toward red. The form had only been a piece of paper, and the paper had been logged on eight stills, and was, for the present and tactical purposes of telling her sister anything, lost.

She wrote in the notebook:

Records room, DISCHARGE 1923 to 1928 cabinet, north drawer: 1924 intake form (Pemberton, Alice Margaret). Discovered 11:47. Photographed (8 stills). Form vanished from top of cabinet between 11:51 and 11:54. Searched records room and administrator's office, all inventoried cabinets in records room, all corners, baseboards, behind/under all cabinets. Not located. Eight stills retained on SD and laptop. Discrepancy noted.

She closed the notebook.

The storm came in earnest at one. The wind howling off the meadow had become the wind that took down the loose slate at the corner of the west wing, audibly, twice: a whip-crack, a long descending scrape, and then nothing. Ray's foreman, on the radio, told her the south corner had given up another six tiles. She told him to clear the perimeter and pull the cones in to the fenceline. She told him she would stay in the records room.

The wind through the records room ceiling rattled like it did after the loose slate had given. The joists above her flexed audibly, twice. The third floor was empty; she had walked it on Day 3. The empty third floor was a hundred and fifty-three years of joists flexed in the only nor'easter that had reached them since closure.

She went to the laptop on the camp chair in the administrator's office, opened it, and verified that the eight stills of the form were still on the hard drive. They were. She opened each one in turn. The patient's name was legible in all eight. The pencil annotation was legible in three. The violet date stamp was legible in two. She copied the eight stills to a second folder, named the folder PEMBERTON_1924_VERIFY, and uploaded a zip of the folder to two cloud accounts that did not share infrastructure. The upload took, in the storm signal, six minutes. The progress bar filled. The upload completed. She closed the laptop.

The Pemberton form had existed long enough for eight photographs and a hundred and two years and now did not exist on this floor of this building. The photographs would have to do. The photographs were going to have to do for a great deal more than a single intake form, she suspected, before this contract finished, but the photographs were what she had.

She did the rest of the empty cabinets. She left the closure era records for another day. She did the records room walls, the records room baseboards, the records room ceiling tile. She found a brass paperclip, two rubber bands, a pencil stub with an eraser end the color of old butter. She did not find the form.

By four, the daylight was the grey with a slight tinge of green of a stormy November Sunday in a nor'easter, which felt more like the no-daylight of an early evening. She turned the headlamp down to medium and walked the corridor between the records room and the foyer. She walked the foyer.

She walked the rear corridor. The chapel-corridor was at forty-six. She did not stay long.

She came back through the rear corridor toward the foyer. She had her hand on the foyer door when the wind in the chapel changed.

The chapel-corridor sound from the day before, the sound she had filed as wind in the chapel intake at the rear sash where the muntin is failing, was the sound the chapel made when wind moved through its broken sash. That sound was a muntin sound. That was a sash sound. That was something she had identified.

The new sound was different.

The new sound was the chapel taking in air. The chapel taking in air was not the same as wind passing through a broken sash. The chapel taking in air was the chapel functioning as a lung, slow, regular, deep. In. Out. The rate of intake was similar to a person breathing. Kate, with her hand on the foyer door, the field notebook in her side pocket, the headlamp on medium, the storm at fifty miles per hour, the field office cold and the form vanished, her mother at second-stage, and the femur in Owens's evidence locker, listened.

She listened for the count of fifteen.

She told herself it was the wind in the chapel.

It was the wind in the chapel. The wind was at fifty miles per hour. The chapel had broken sashes on three sides and a slate roof in poor condition and a 1947 connecting corridor that opened directly into the central administration. The chapel functioning as a lung in a fifty-mile wind was, in any reasonable architectural read, an expected occurrence.

She was right.

She was also right that it sounded like a person breathing.

She wrote in the notebook:

Chapel-corridor, 16:14: sustained respiratory sound, slow regular interval (~3 sec), deep. Reading: wind through broken sash and slate, exterior compromised by storm. Reading: confirmed. Note: sounds like a person breathing.

She closed the notebook.

She let herself out through the front door, locked it, and walked through the rain to the car. The wreckers' equipment in the gravel lot was tarped against the wind. The trailer light was off; Ray and his foreman had gone home.

She got into the Outback. She did not turn the engine on for the count of thirty. The dashboard, when she turned the key, glowed: clock, fuel gauge, the field thermometer at thirty-seven outside, the inside reading the rapidly cooling fifty-eight of a vehicle parked in a nor'easter for six hours.

She put the car in gear.

ARCHIVE EXCERPT

Letter from Estelle Doran to her sister · smuggled out · June 1961

Dear Beth –

They have given me what they call the calming. I cannot feel my left hand. Marie was taken yesterday and has not come back. If you do not hear from me again by August, do not believe what they tell you about what happened. The doctor here is named Kessler. The other one. The young one is worse than the old one and the old one signs everything. Tell Mama I am still myself. Don't write back to this address. The mail is read.

– E.

CHAPTER SEVEN

Eleanor

Day 6

"Tell Mama I am still myself."
— Estelle Doran, smuggled letter from Marston Hill, June 1961

The flowers were yellow because Margaret had said yellow.

The supermarket in town had three buckets of cut flowers in the cooler at the front: white roses, pink carnations, yellow chrysanthemums. The chrysanthemums were the only yellow on offer that morning. She bought a bunch, paid the cashier in cash because she was carrying it for the trip, and got back in the Outback. The drive into town was eleven miles in remnant rain, the kind of rain a nor'easter's tail laid down on the morning after, half mist and half drip, and the wipers on the Outback were one season older than they should be.

Tessa Ross's apartment was at the end of the second corridor of the assisted-living residence at the south edge of town. Eleanor's apartment was next door. The arrangement was not typical for assisted-living arrangements, but the registry call sheet had been clear: when contracted state work needed access to Eleanor Ross, the contact person was the granddaughter, in the next apartment, who had been her grandmother's primary caregiver for two years and would be for whatever time was left.

Tessa opened her own apartment door before Kate had knocked. She was twenty-six and tall and had been on her feet since five. It was the second-year nursing student's posture, which Kate had seen before, as if the person had not yet learned to sit at work.

"Welton."

"Ross."

"Tessa, please."

"Tessa. Kate."

"Granny's good today. She'll talk. She's expecting you. The flowers."

She took them from Kate without ceremony and put them in a cup of water she had set out on the counter. The cup was a child's enamel cup from the seventies with a cartoon rabbit on it, the kind of cup that lived on a kitchen windowsill and did not have a parent vessel to match it. Tessa returned with a smaller arrangement, five chrysanthemums, the rest set aside for the apartment.

"Half stays here. Half goes to Granny. She doesn't keep flowers more than two days; they confuse her."

"I see."

"Coffee? She drinks it black with one sugar. I'll make a pot for her. How do you drink it, Kate?"

"Black is fine."

They went next door. Tessa knocked twice, called “Granny,” opened the door before there was a response. The apartment beyond was a one-bedroom with a view of the parking lot. Eleanor was in an armchair by the window with a blanket over her knees and the morning paper folded to the crossword. She had her glasses on. Her hair, which was white, was pulled back in a clip Kate did not see most women her age wearing.

"Eleanor Ross."

"Kate Welton. The architect."

"Kate. Sit down."

Kate sat in the chair Tessa indicated, a wooden chair set across from the armchair at a distance Kate read as the distance Eleanor preferred for people she did not yet have a measure of. Tessa came in with the coffee, put one cup beside Eleanor and one beside Kate, sat herself on the bed, and folded her hands.

"Tessa stays?" Kate asked.

"Tessa stays. She's writing it down for me. I forget." Eleanor's voice was careful and slightly slow, the librarian's careful and the nurse's careful at the same time. "What do you want to know."

"I'm documenting the building. Doing a closure-eve survey. I'm here for fourteen days, of which I have eight left. The state hires me for my architecture expertise. The architecture is what I came to talk to you about. Where rooms were. Floor plans we can verify against the building. That kind of thing. And the basement."

"The hydrotherapy basement."

"Yes."

A small pause.

Eleanor's hand on the armrest tightened by a small amount. Kate registered it.

"We'll get to the basement. Not yet."

"Okay."

"Tell me what you want first."

"Tell me the eighties."

Eleanor took a sip of her coffee. The cup was the kind with two handles, a hospital cup the assisted-living staff had probably kept from one of her hospital visits. Her hands shook by a small amount with the cup. Tessa had her notebook open on her lap.

"The eighties was the Thorazine era, mostly. Some of the older patients were still on what we used to call the calming, which was paraldehyde, which had been off the market for ten years by then but had been kept in the basement of the pharmacy in a lockbox that Theo had the key to. It was used on what the staff called the difficult ones. Soft restraints were Posey vests on the upper floors and leather wrist straps with sheepskin lining on the lower. Stelazine and Haldol on rotation. Lithium for the manic patients. The staff was supposed to draw blood for the lithium levels weekly but on the women's wing the levels got drawn when somebody had time, which was less than weekly. That meant the levels got out of range, which meant the patient got worse, and Theo would write it up as deterioration following good-faith treatment."

She set the cup down.

"Documentation. The chart system was supposed to be physician orders signed by the prescribing physician, then by the duty nurse, then by the head nurse on second sign, then countersigned by the medical director on the morning following. Five signatures. By the late eighties Theo was signing four of them. He was writing the orders, signing the orders, signing the duty-nurse line, and countersigning his own countersignature. He gave the head nurse line to me to sign because I did not say no when he asked me to sign things."

"Which is what you wanted to tell me."

"It is."

"What you couldn't say at the time."

"I had three children at the time. I'm eighty-one years old. The man is dead. I'm telling it now because I have nothing left to fear."

Eleanor sat back. Tessa was writing. The pen made the small scritching sound of a good pen on good notebook paper.

"Theodore had a son."

"Wendell."

"Wendell. Fifty-seven now. He was at the hospital during the summer from sixteen on. He interned in '88. Kate, you have my permission to hear about the architecture and the protocols. I won't speak of the son further. Not today."

"Understood."

"You'll have it soon. Not today."

A pause. Eleanor looked at the window. The rain on the parking-lot side had started to fall heavier. The cars in the lot had their lights on and Kate counted three from where she sat.

"Wendell's father was a careful man," Eleanor said. "Never crossed lines you could see."

She paused. Kate did not interrupt.

"The lines you could see," Eleanor said, slower. "He never crossed those."

"And the ones you couldn't."

"Those, well, he was the line."

A long beat.

Tessa had stopped writing. Kate had not picked up her cup. Eleanor looked at the window again. The rain on the parking lot kept coming.

"Granny."

"I'm alright, Tessa-pet. Take it down."

Tessa took it down.

"The architecture," Kate said, after the beat the conversation needed. "Tell me what I have to know that I'll not learn from the floor plans."

"The chapel-corridor."

"Cold."

"It was cold when it was built and it has been cold since. I don't know what makes it cold. I worked on the third floor in the winters of '77 and '78, before I made head nurse, and I would walk through the chapel-corridor on the way to the back ward and I would always feel it. Theo said it was the slate. The slate is part of it."

"What's the rest of it."

"I don't know. Probably because I've stopped trying to know. The chapel-corridor is what it is. Don't stand in it longer than your work requires."

"I won't."

"The east-wing service stair."

"Sealed at the landing."

"In '57. They sealed it because a patient came down at three in the morning of a winter Sunday and walked out the front door. They said. The patient was Marie Doran, who I never met. The staircase was sealed and what was on the stairs was sealed with it. I'd tell you what is on the stairs if I knew."

"Okay."

"The chamber between 2-E and 2-D."

A beat.

"Yes," Kate said.

"You found it."

"I found it on the IR on Day 3."

"There was a chamber there in '68 when I started. You have it on your IR. I was never told what was in it. I knew the room was there. I didn't know what was inside."

"That's okay."

"The basement."

"Tell me about the basement."

Eleanor told her about the basement. She told her about the sequence of doors, the way the deadbolts were stacked on the inside of the third door so a person who let themselves in could not be locked in by someone above. The shock equipment had been dismantled in '86 but the cabinet behind the duty desk had not. She told her about Theo's habit of doing his own basement rounds. She told Kate about the bolt on the outside of the door. She did not tell Kate why the bolt mattered. The bolt was, on the surface of her telling, a piece of architectural information.

A bolt on the outside of a basement door in a Kirkbride asylum was a piece of equipment that had been designed to keep someone inside that basement. The bolt was a piece of architectural information that was also, on the second take, not architectural information at all. Eleanor wasn't telling Kate about a bolt. Eleanor was, in the tone of a woman who had told her granddaughter on a Tuesday morning to fetch a sweater, telling Kate that a bolt existed and was on the outside of a door. Kate took it down.

It was eleven thirty-eight when Tessa stood up to refill the coffee. Eleanor's hand made a small wave that meant no more coffee. Kate stood up.

"Eleanor."

"Kate."

"Thank you."

"Come back. There will be more. I'll lose some of it before you do."

"I'll come back."

"Tomorrow."

"Day after tomorrow. Tomorrow I have a chamber to open."

A pause.

"Kate."

"Yes."

"Come closer."

Kate crouched beside the chair.

Eleanor's hand came up and caught her at the wrist. The grip was old-nurse's grip, which was a grip that had taken blood pressure readings on six thousand patients and could find a pulse through a wool sweater.

"Don't go into hydrotherapy basement alone."

A beat.

"Why."

Eleanor looked at her. The pause was longer this time. Eleanor's eyes went to the window, came back, went to Kate's face.

"I can't remember," she sounded sad.

A long beat.

"That's alright"

"I knew this morning. I did not write it down before I forgot. I should have written it down. Tessa-pet, I should have written it down."

"It's alright, Granny."

"It is not alright."

Eleanor's grip on Kate's wrist did not loosen.

"Kate. Don't."

"I'll wait until I have a reason."

"You'll have a reason. Don't."

"I won't."

Eleanor let her wrist go.

Kate stood. Tessa walked her to the door of the apartment. They did not speak in the corridor. At the door of Tessa's apartment Tessa stopped and faced Kate.

"What did she remember this morning?"

"She didn't tell me. She wrote it down. The notebook is on her kitchen table. I haven't read it. She hasn't asked me to. She might want it."

"Yes."

"She knows things. She does not always know that she knows them."

"Yes."

"You'll come back."

"I will."

"After what she just said, you'll come back."

"I will."

Tessa nodded. Kate left.

The drive back through the rain was eleven miles. The rain came back full halfway through and the wipers on the Outback failed at a stop sign and started again at the next one. Kate drove at the speed of someone squinting through a windshield that wasn't quite clear. She did not turn the radio on.

She was thinking about the sentence: those, he was the line. She filed it away in her mind. It was all information. The forgetting was information; the line was information; the not-yet-confessable son was information; the eight children Eleanor had not borne but had failed to protect on Theo's ward were information. The work for the day, the architectural work, was inside her now alongside the rest of the work. She had stopped believing, on the drive back, that the architectural work and the rest of the work were two different jobs.

By the time she pulled into the gravel lot at Marston Hill the rain had become the kind of rain that came down at a forty-five-degree angle and was not going to stop in time for the wreckers' Friday.

Ray was at the trailer. He had a sandwich. He raised it.

"Eleanor."

"Eleanor."

"How was it?"

"She had something to tell me. She forgot what."

"Still worth the trip?"

"Definitely. She didn’t forget everything."

"Yeah."

"Yeah."

She went into the building.

She did not go to the field office. She went up the central stairs to the second floor of the east wing and stood outside the door of Ward 2-E for three minutes. She went down to the field office, took out her notebook, and wrote down everything Eleanor had said, in her own block-letter handwriting, with the date and the time.

By two in the afternoon she had finished the IR survey of the third floor of the west wing, which had not given her anything new, and she had photographed the chapel-corridor from both ends, which had also not given her anything new, and the day was running out the way short November days ran out at a latitude with a partially-clouded sky after a nor'easter. Ray had rebuilt the cone perimeter on the gravel lot. The rain had stopped at one. The wreckers were on the schedule for staging Friday for a Monday start. The time moved inexorably forward.

CHAPTER EIGHT

The file that won't stay put

Day 7

"There can be no doubt that the consciousness of the rapid increase of my superstition served mainly to accelerate the increase itself."
— Edgar Allan Poe, "The Fall of the House of Usher" (1839)

Kate went into the chapel at six forty-three. The Pemberton form was on the altar.

The chapel had been on her schedule for Day 6, and she had not done the chapel on Day 6 because she had been with Eleanor and then driven eleven-miles in remnant rain with bad windshield wipers. The chapel moved on her schedule to first thing on Day 7. At six forty-three she had come up the rear corridor of the central administration with the headlamp on the low setting and the camp blanket folded under one arm and the field bag at her hip and pushed the inner door of the chapel-corridor open.

The chapel-corridor read forty-six.

She did not stay in the chapel-corridor. She crossed it at the speed of a person who had already paid attention to a forty-six-degree corridor four mornings running and had nothing to add about it. She came to the chapel door. The chapel door was original 1873 oak with a wrought-iron pull on a strap hinge, unlocked, ajar by three inches. She pulled it open.

She had observed the chapel in the photographs and the floor plan a dozen times. Twenty-two pews on each side of a central aisle, varnished oak gone to dust over a hundred and twenty years of salt air through the slate. A small organ had been removed in '94, leaving a square absence in the floor where the bench stood. A baptismal font at the front was dry. A wooden lectern. An altar. A stained-glass window above the altar in the simple geometric pattern Kirkbride architects favored over figurative work, the leading gone soft at the bottom where the storm had pushed water through the casement on the south side. The pews on the south side carried a fine line of rainwater along their feet that had not yet dried. The slate roof had held everywhere except above the third pew on the south, where a steady drip the size of a thimble had come down through the night and which Kate logged at six forty-five.

On the altar was the 1924 intake form for Pemberton, Alice Margaret.

She stood in the chapel doorway. Her tablet read forty-six. The wind was not up.

Six fifty-one.

She walked up the central aisle. She walked at the speed of a person who was about to do work she did not want to do. The aisle was twenty feet. She had her hand on the handle of the field bag at her hip. The blanket was over her shoulder. The headlamp was on low.

She reached the altar.

The form was the 1924 intake form Kate had photographed and lost on Day 5. The same form. On the altar.

It was lying face up, flat.

It was lying in the center of the altar with its long axis running east to west, which was the direction the altar ran, and the violet date stamp at the top right was visible and the pencil annotation at the side were visible at three feet. The paper had not been folded since she last saw it. The paper had not, by the look of it, been moved by hand.

She stood at the altar.

She had her gloves on already. She had put them on at the chapel door without thinking about it. She raised the Pentax. She took eight stills: a wide, two mediums, three close, one of the pencil annotation, and one of the date stamp. She lowered the camera. She did not pick the form up. She did not put a hand on the form. She did not move the form an inch.

She wrote in the notebook:

Chapel, central altar, 06:51: 1924 intake form (Pemberton, Alice Margaret), face up, flat, long axis E-W. Form vanished from records room cabinet on Day 5 at 11:54. Interval: 67 hours. Location: chapel altar, 38 feet south of central administration through chapel-corridor. Photographed (8 stills). Will not move at this time.

She closed the notebook.

She stood at the altar.

Alice Margaret Pemberton had been twenty-one years old. Alice Margaret Pemberton had been committed by her husband Charles W. Pemberton on March 14, 1924, for moral insanity, hysteric tendencies, and the refusal of conjugal duties. Alice Margaret Pemberton had been admitted to the East Wing, Ward 2-E. Alice Margaret Pemberton had spent two years at Bryn Mawr before her husband withdrew her support.

Alice Margaret Pemberton had died at the institution in 1931, age 28. The official record of cause of death described exhaustion following infection, by the hand of a man who had committed her to the institution and which the institution had not asked any further questions about.

The form did not say any of this. The form said the first paragraph. The rest Kate had pulled from the deputy archivist's intake which had she had been able to pull forward to today. The dossier had arrived on the laptop at five thirty-eight that morning. Kate had read it once at six and would review it again.

Kate Margaret Welton was thirty-eight years old. Kate Margaret Welton had not been a wife to anyone. Kate Margaret Welton had spent six years at Cornell and Penn and had not had her support withdrawn by anyone, because she had never had any support to withdraw. Kate Margaret Welton was articulate. Kate Margaret Welton was, on some accounting, difficult. Kate Margaret Welton's middle name had been her grandmother's name on her mother's side, and her mother's name was Margaret, and Margaret was on a memory care wing three states south, in a unit that did not warm up before noon, and the morning was unraveling into a thing Kate could not control.

She walked back down the aisle and sat in the third pew on the left, halfway between the altar and the chapel door. She did not turn the headlamp off. The chapel was at sixty-six now. The chapel-corridor was at forty-six. The interior of the chapel at this hour was the same temperature as the rear corridor of the central administration; only the chapel-corridor between them was cold.

The phone in her pocket rang at seven oh four.

Mom.

She took it out. She let the screen ring through the count of three, decided, and answered.

"Hi, Mom."

"Lila? Is that you?"

A beat.

Margaret on her bad days had a different voice than Margaret on her good days, and the voice on the other end of the phone was the bad-day voice. The careful librarian rhythm was missing. The slight dryness was missing. Instead, there was the voice of a woman who had been alive for seventy-one years and who had at this hour lost six hundred and thirty months of those years and who was, for reasons that were not Kate's to ask about, talking to her older sister, who had died of breast cancer in 1972 at the age of thirty-one.

"It's Kate, Mom."

"Lila. Where have you been? It's been such a long time."

"Mom."

"I called your house. The number doesn't work. I called the school. They said you weren't there. Lila, why has it been such a long time?"

A beat.

"Mom. It's Kate. It's your daughter Kate. I'm in Maine on a contract. Joanne is twenty minutes from you. She'll come over if you'd like."

"Lila, where have you been?"

Kate decided in the third pew of an 1873 chapel forty feet south of the central administration of Marston Hill State Hospital with a 1924 intake form on the altar in front of her and a headlamp on low at her shoulder and the chapel temperature reading sixty-six. The decision was that she would not correct Margaret on this call. She would be Lila.

She had read the literature. She had argued with Joanne about it. The literature on Alzheimer's was clear that you did not orient a person with severe disorientation back to the present; you met them where they were. The orientation was violence. Kate had agreed with the literature in principle and never been required to live that principle until this morning.

"Margaret," she said. "I've been working in another state. I'm sorry I haven't called more often."

"Oh, honey. Where are you."

"I'm at a hospital. I'm working at a hospital, Margaret."

"You're a nurse?"

"I'm a kind of nurse."

"You always were."

For forty minutes, Kate sat in the chapel and was Lila. She talked to her mother about the kitchen of the house in 1956 where Margaret had grown up. She agreed with her mother that the bus to the high school took longer than it had to. She remembered, on her mother's behalf, the year that the dog ran away. She agreed that yes, she had been out of touch, and yes, it had been her fault, and yes, she would call more often. She let the dead Lila speak through her own voice for forty minutes. The dead Lila said the things to her sister that Kate had no way of knowing the dead Lila had said in 1972 or had not said before she stopped being able to say anything. Margaret, on the other end of the phone, listened and asked questions and did not, for forty minutes, suspect anything.

At seven forty-four, Margaret, in her own kitchen three states south, asked if Lila could come for dinner.

"I can't tonight, Margaret. I'm working."

"Alright, honey. Soon, though."

"Soon."

"I love you."

"I love you too, Margaret."

She hung up.

She sat in the pew. She did not turn the headlamp off. The chapel did not move. The drip on the third pew of the south side dripped once, twice, again. The floor of the chapel was the cold-floor of a November morning forty feet south of a building with the heat off. She had been Lila for forty-one minutes. She had a sister, in another sense, on the altar in front of her, twenty-eight years old when the institution had stopped recording her. She had not expected to experience this much resonance on the job. It felt heavy.

After a count of a hundred, she stood up. She walked up the central aisle at the speed of a woman returning to plumb. She came to the altar.

The form was gone.

She had photographed it. It was there at six fifty-one. It was now seven forty-five and the form was no longer on the altar. The altar was a flat oak surface with a slight depression in the center where the missal had sat for a hundred and twenty years, and a fine dust at the edges. The form was not on the altar. The form was not under the altar. The form was not in the missal-shaped depression. The form was not on any of the pews she walked back through, and she did walk back through them, all forty-four pews, with the headlamp on full.

She did not bother looking for very long.

She came to the chapel door at seven fifty-three. She stopped on the threshold and checked her tablet.

The chapel itself was at sixty-six degrees, which was the same as the rear corridor of the central administration. The chapel-corridor between the chapel and the rear corridor of the central administration was at forty-six.

Kate realized the chapel-corridor was always forty-six. It had been forty-six on Day 1, when the rear corridor had been sixty-one and the differential had been fifteen. It had been forty-six on Day 4 at seven oh two, when the rear corridor had been sixty-one and the differential had been fifteen. It had been forty-six in a fifty-mile gust on Day 5 with the rear corridor dropping a degree an hour. It was forty-six now, at seven fifty-three on a clear Tuesday morning, with the rear corridor at sixty-six and the differential, today, twenty.

The differential moved. The chapel-corridor did not.

She wrote in the notebook:

Chapel, 07:53: ambient sixty-six (matches rear corridor). Chapel-corridor: forty-six (sustained). Form on altar at 06:51 (photographed); form gone from altar at 07:45. Interval: 54 minutes. Will not search further at this time.

She closed the notebook.

She crossed the chapel-corridor at the speed of a person who had been warned not to linger.

She went back to the field office.

She was on Day 7 of a fourteen-day contract.

She had seven days of light.

The form's eight stills from Day 5 were on the laptop. The form's eight stills from this morning were on the SD card in the Pentax. She uploaded the new stills to the same two cloud accounts as the Day 5 stills. She named the folder PEMBERTON_1924_VERIFY_2.

She closed the laptop.

She did not call Joanne. She would call Joanne tonight, from the motel, with a glass of water, and would tell her the parts she could, but would not tell her the part where Lila came for dinner. The part where Lila came for dinner would stay with Kate.

She did not call Margaret again.

She put the kettle on the camp stove for tea, because the field office at eight in the morning of Day 7 was sixty-one degrees and the heated vest on its highest setting was at fifteen percent battery, and the thing she needed next was a hot drink and a clean field notebook page and an architectural detail to look at that was not a piece of paper that came and went.

She made tea.

She drank it sitting at the table under the south window, with the laptop closed, the field notebook closed, and the lap blanket over her knees, watching the meadow come back into focus through the residual fog. The chicory was flat. The dock was flat. The crows from the cemetery beech had not come back yet.

After the tea she opened the field notebook again. She turned to the first blank page after the morning's notation. She wrote:

Day 7. Form located, chapel altar, 06:51. Form vanished, chapel altar, between 07:04 and 07:45 (during phone call). Eleanor: do not enter hydrotherapy basement alone. Margaret: bad day, mistook me for Lila, 40 min sustained on call. Tomorrow: cut crew opens E-W chamber on Day 8 cut order, partition 2-D / 2-E.

She closed the notebook.

She turned the heated vest off, swapped to the second M12 battery from the case, turned it back on and set it to medium.

She got up. The chapel was where the day's work waited. She had eight more pews to photograph, and the chapel-corridor temperature anomaly to log a sixth time, and a chamber to oversee the cutting of in twenty-six hours.

She went back to the chapel.

CHAPTER NINE

The wall comes down

Day 8 · morning

"Nothing is so painful to the human mind as a great and sudden change."
— Mary Wollstonecraft Shelley, Frankenstein (1818)

Ray had brought Voss in for the cut.

Bill Voss was the cut foreman from the regional contractor's specialized team, twenty years of cuts on his book, and Ray had asked for him personally rather than put his own crew on a cut where they would not yet know what they were cutting into. Kate had filed the cut order on Day 6 and re-stamped it on Day 7 with Voss's signature, and she had walked the partition between Ward 2-D and Ward 2-E with Ray on Day 7 evening to show him the tape. The blue tape was still there. No one had moved it.

At eight thirty she was at the trailer with Ray and his foreman Doug. Ray would not be running the saw; that was the point of bringing in Voss. Ray would be in the corridor with Kate. Doug would run support for Voss. Marcus, who had been on Ray's crew for eight years, would handle the cordon and the dust.

"Welton."

"Mendez."

"You ready."

"I'm ready."

"You want me to call this off."

"No."

He had asked her three times that morning. She had answered the same way three times. The cut was on the order, the order was on the schedule, the schedule was on the wall of the trailer in Ray's handwriting, and the cut was at nine. They were going to make the cut.

By eight forty-five they were on the second floor of the east wing. The corridor lights were on. The fluorescents had warmed up enough to be even, finally, after a week and a half of cycling in. Voss had arrived at eight ten with his own crew of two, the four-inch core, the dust shroud, and a shop vac the size of a barrel. Kate had not met him before Day 7. The crew was geared: hard hats, eye protection, N95s, hearing protection.

"Welton."

"Voss."

"I have your order. Pilot core, four inches, center of the marked rectangle, depth to refusal, hold for survey supervisor."

"Center of the marked rectangle. Yes."

"And after the pilot."

"After the pilot, hold. We assess. I'll make the next call."

At nine oh two Voss set the saw against the plaster at the center of Kate's blue rectangle. The saw was a Hilti core drill with an eight-millimeter water feed. The water was the kind of detail that mattered for asbestos suppression, which was why this cut was scheduled and recorded. Voss started the bit and the bit started turning and the plaster started coming off in a wet slurry into the shop vac.

The bit went in. Plaster, then brick, brick, more brick. The bit was through plaster at one inch. The bit was through the first course of 1923 brick at six inches. The bit was through the second course of 1923 brick at fourteen. At sixteen inches the resistance stopped.

Voss stopped the bit. The depth gauge said sixteen. The bit had gone through about fifteen inches of resistance and then the resistance had ceased, the way resistance ceased when the bit broke through into a cavity. He pulled the bit back. The bit came back slick with water and gray slurry and a faint dry dust that was not the dust of any cut Voss had run that year.

Voss looked at Kate.

"Cavity, Welton."

"Cavity."

"Hold."

"Hold."

Voss stepped back. Kate stepped forward.

She had brought the inspection camera. The inspection camera was a small flexible-tip articulating bore, longer than the borescope they had used in the morgue, with its own LED ring and a four-inch screen. She fed the camera into the four-inch pilot core. She had her gloves on. The camera went in. The screen lit up.

The cavity was finished. The plaster on the inner faces had been troweled smooth. Someone had built a room and then sealed it up.

The room had a floor. The floor was wooden, varnished, dust coated.

The room had a chair. The chair was wooden, hand-carved, with a high back. It was placed at the east end of the cavity, facing west, toward the camera.

The chair had restraints. The restraints were leather, the leather of an old institution, worn smooth, buckled at the wrist points and the ankle points and the chest point. Sheepskin lining at the wrist points.

The chair was occupied.

Kate moved the camera by the count of one degree at a time and the woman in the chair came into the frame.

The remains were desiccated. The skin had pulled tight over the bone. The hair on the skull was the color hair was when it had been on a skull for a long time. It was a color Kate had seen before. The hands were on the arms of the chair. The wrists were buckled. The ankles, where the camera could see them, were buckled. The chest was buckled.

She had been alive when they had buckled her in.

Kate did not let herself follow that further than the one sentence.

She pulled the camera out of the four-inch hole.

She took out the field notebook. She wrote:

Patient A1, East Chamber, located 09:42. Wooden chair, high back, hand-carved. Leather restraints, three-point: wrists, ankles, chest. Sheepskin lining at wrist contact. Adult female remains, desiccated, seated, hands tied. Inner cavity dimensions per camera: 8 ft x 3 ft. Plaster intact, finished. Partition between Ward 2-E and Ward 2-D. Will document fully on opening.

She named her A1. She did not name her by the name on the form. The name on the form was the name of a woman whose form Kate had photographed twice and lost twice, and the woman in the chair could not be named without an identification, and an identification was not the survey supervisor's job.

There was, in the photographs on her laptop and the photographs on the SD card and the zipped folders on two cloud accounts, a 1924 intake form for a woman who had been twenty-one and articulate and committed by a husband to East Wing, Ward 2-E. There was, in this chair, in this cavity, on the other side of the partition between Ward 2-D and Ward 2-E, a woman of an age at death the forensic anthropology would establish in the next forty-eight hours. The two might be the same woman. The two might not. Kate, on Day 8 at nine forty-six, would not be the person to make the match.

She closed the notebook.

She turned to Voss.

"Open the rectangle. Carefully. I want a four-by-six opening in the center, no more. We're not extracting today. We are documenting."

"Yes."

"And the inner plaster face. There is a sealed inner face. The chamber is plastered on the inside. I want that face left intact for now."

"Yes."

"I'll core through the inner face myself when I'm ready."

"Yes."

Voss nodded. He went back to the saw.

Kate left the corridor. She walked at her own pace down the central stair to the ground floor and out the front door of the central administration and across the gravel toward the trailer and then turned at the trailer step and crossed the gravel to the back of the trailer where the cone perimeter met the chain-link fence.

She vomited.

She had not eaten. There was nothing to bring up. She brought up the coffee from six and bile and water. Her hand was on the chain-link and her boots were in the gravel and her vest was on medium and she was thirty-eight years old and on Day 8 of a fourteen-day contract and the woman in the chair would have been twenty-one when they buckled her in to the chair.

Ray came around the corner of the trailer. He had a bottle of water in his hand. He did not say anything. He held the bottle out. Kate took it. She rinsed her mouth, spat into the gravel, drank a small swallow, gave it back. He took it and capped it.

"Welton."

"Mendez."

"Take ten."

"Ten."

"I'll have Voss hold."

She sat on the gravel with her back against the chain-link fence breathing slowly and staring at nothing. Ray went back to the second floor of the east wing to tell Voss to hold.

The November sun came through the walnut trees and dropped patches of light on the gravel that moved as the wind moved the branches. The patches of light moved across her boots, and Kate sat with her back to the fence and the bottle of water on the gravel beside her.

A blue jay came out of the walnut crowns at the south end of the lot, took one slow flap across the meadow, and was gone behind the chapel roof. The wind moved the orange traffic cones at the gate. Her vest was on medium because the work she was doing was usually the kind of work she did sitting still.

After a few minutes, she stood up.

She stood up the same way she had stood up in the morgue on Day 4 after the three-minute count, which was the way of a level returning to plumb, and she walked back to the central administration and up the central stair and into the corridor. The cut crew was standing six feet back from the cut with their hands on their tools.

"Voss."

"Welton."

"Open it."

"Yes."

He opened it. The four-by-six opening took twenty minutes with the core saw running on the perimeter and the shop vac taking the slurry. The crew cleared the cut debris into bags. The opening was done. The inner plaster face of the chamber was visible through the opening, intact, finished as it had been when the chamber was sealed.

Kate stepped to the opening with the inspection camera and the small core bit. She breached the inner plaster face with a one-inch hole at the center. She inserted the camera. She photographed the chamber methodically, in a slow corkscrew, the way Ray had photographed the morgue duct on Day 4. Forty-six stills.

She did not enter the chamber.

She did not move the chair.

She did not touch the woman.

She closed the cut at the inner face with a temporary seal of clear plastic the cut crew kept for openings like these. She had Voss put a hard cordon around the opening and tape the corridor at both ends. She told Ray to call the county forensic line. He had already done it. Owens was on her way.

The time on Kate's tablet was eleven oh seven.

She wrote in the field notebook:

Patient A1 documented at 11:07. 46 stills. Chamber sealed with temporary plastic at inner face per protocol. Cut foreman: Voss. Forensic team called at 09:51, ETA 13:00. Will not extract until forensic team on-site.

She closed the notebook.

She went down to the trailer. She drank water. She ate half a granola bar. The granola bar was the kind that came twelve to a box at the gas station off Route 8.

She finished the granola bar. She ate a second one. She drank a second bottle of water.

By the time Owens arrived at one fifty-one, Kate was on her third granola bar and her hand had stopped shaking.

She had a job to do.

Owens came up the central stair with Hector and three uniformed forensic technicians at one in the afternoon. They brought a fold-up table the size of a coffin. The kind of measured movement Kate had seen in Owens on Day 4 only doubled. They went to the corridor. They went to the opening. They stood at the temporary plastic seal Kate had had Voss tape across the cut, and Owens examined the seal before she turned to Kate.

"Welton."

"Owens."

"Walk me through what you found."

Kate walked her through it.

By the time Kate had finished her walkthrough, Hector had unfolded the table in the corridor, the technicians had set up the lights, and the cordon was being widened by another six feet. Voss stood at the corridor end with his hands in his pockets. Ray stood beside him. The fluorescents in the corridor were on full and the corridor was at fifty-eight degrees, two below the rest of the building, because Voss's saw had been running for two hours and the dust shroud had pulled cold air in from the chapel-corridor through a route that, on the floor plan, did not exist.

The chapel-corridor was at forty-six.

It had been at forty-six on Day 1.

It had been at forty-six this morning at six.

It was at forty-six now.

Kate logged the reading and said nothing, the way she had handled every reading from the chapel-corridor.

Owens turned to her. "I'll need an hour to set up. After that we open."

"Yes."

"You stay in the corridor. You don’t need to be in the room."

"Okay."

"Welton."

"Yes."

"You did this work properly. I want you to know that. The chamber is intact because of how you ran the cut."

"Thank you."

Owens went to her table. Kate went to the corridor's south end and sat on the linoleum with her back to the wall. The wall was a wall in a building that was coming down in six days, and the woman she had named A1 was through the wall behind her. The cut crew was waiting.

The fluorescents above her flickered once and steadied. Her tablet measured the corridor at fifty-eight. The chamber, on the other side of the partition, would log warmer in the hour Owens would be working in it under the field lights, and would log warmer still by the time the body left the chamber on a litter at four. By Day 14 the chamber would be a piece of evidentiary material under tarp on a flatbed. By Day 15 the woman in the chair would be the woman in the state lab. By Day 14 there would, on the page, be a name.

CHAPTER TEN

The body is recent

Day 8 · evening

"The past is never dead. It's not even past."
— William Faulkner, Requiem for a Nun (1951)

By two thirty Owens had aged the morning find at approximately one hundred years.

She had said it standing in the corridor of the second floor of the east wing in front of the four-by-six opening Kate had Voss cut at eleven, her assistant Hector in the room behind her with the kit, the chamber sealed in clear plastic the way Kate had sealed it. Her tone was the foreman's tone Owens used for an estimate she would not need to revise.

"Ninety years, plus or minus ten. Female. Twenties to thirties. The chair is original 1923. The leather of the restraints is older than the chair, possibly state-asylum issue from 1900 to 1920. The sheepskin lining is original. Cause of death pending the autopsy, but the absence of acute trauma to the visible skeleton suggests, at first look, that she was buckled in alive and wasn't extracted from the chair in the chamber."

"Okay."

"Welton."

"Yes."

"I'm going to extract her this afternoon. I have authorization from the state."

"Yes."

"I want you to be in the corridor when we do. I don't want you in the room."

"Alright."

"have not the survey supervisor. You stay in the corridor. You log what I tell you to log. We extract under your survey."

"Yes."

She did not argue. She had argued with Owens once, on Day 4 in the morgue, when Kate had wanted to handle the femur and Owens had said no, and Kate had said yes, and Owens had said no, and Kate had relented. She did not argue today.

By three Owens and Hector and the three technicians had widened the opening to a full doorway, four feet by seven, and the chamber was open to the corridor. The chair was visible from the corridor at fifteen feet. The technicians had laid down protective sheeting on the corridor floor leading to the cordon, and a fold-up table for the body, and a smaller table for the restraints once Owens cut them at the buckles. Hector was running the camera. Owens was in the room with the chair. Kate was in the corridor at the south end with the field notebook open and her gloves on.

"Wrist restraint, left," Owens said. "Cutting the buckle."

"Wrist restraint, left, cut at buckle, fifteen oh seven," Kate wrote.

"Wrist restraint, right."

"Right, fifteen oh nine."

"Ankle, left."

"Ankle, left, fifteen eleven."

"Ankle, right."

"Right, fifteen thirteen."

"Chest."

"Chest, fifteen fifteen."

The buckles came off the leather one at a time, each with the small dry click of leather a hundred and a few years old releasing from a brass tongue worn smooth by the same number of years. Each one Hector photographed before Owens cut it. Each one went into a bag with a tag with a chain-of-custody number Kate also logged. The restraints were treated with a courtesy a state forensic team gave to evidentiary material that would, if the chain held, eventually go in front of a state attorney. Kate had been around the courtesy on Day 4 with the femur. Today the courtesy was being given to the leather of an institution that had buckled in a young woman a hundred years ago and not unbuckled her.

By four thirty the chair had been disassembled, the restraints had been cut at the buckles and bagged separately, the woman had been laid out on the sterile sheet on the folding table, and the table had been set in the middle of the corridor where the field lights had the most reach. Kate, in the corridor, did her own documentation against Owens's protocol. Hector with the camera, Owens with the gloves, Voss, Marcus, and Ray in the corridor at the north end, observing.

At four forty-three Hector said: "Renata."

Owens looked up from the body on the table.

"Behind. Behind the chair seat. There is a... it goes back. There is another cavity."

Owens was at the back wall of the chamber inside ten seconds. She put her hand against the plaster. She did the rap test Kate had done on Day 2 in the corridor outside Ward 2-E, knuckle to plaster, listening for the change in resonance. The plaster gave back a hollow echo.

"Voss."

"Yes."

"I need that wall opened. Now. Same protocol as this morning."

"Yes."

Voss cut. Kate stood in the corridor. Ray stood beside her. The plaster came down at the back of the chamber, the inner face of a wall behind a wall, the second skin of a chamber that had been built behind another chamber.

The cut took twelve minutes.

Behind the chamber was another cavity.

The other cavity was small. It was the size of a closet, eight feet long, eighteen inches wide, brick on the back face, plaster on the front face.

Inside the other cavity was a body.

Owens, behind the cut, said: "Welton."

"Yes."

"Step back."

Kate stepped back.

The body in the second cavity was not desiccated. This body was wrapped in clear sheeting that was water-stained at the bottom and dry at the top. The body appeared to be a woman in her late thirties. The face was visible through the sheeting and the face was recognizable.

It was a face Kate had seen around.

It was the face from the deli counter at the supermarket in town, on the pre-survey trip Kate had taken two and a half years ago, when she had been in town for a week to pull the federal-survey set and walk the building's exterior. The woman had been in line in front of her and had ordered a half pound of pepper turkey and a quarter pound of provolone, and the deli clerk had said the provolone was almost out and the woman had said pepper jack was fine. It was the face from the gas station off Route 8 the next morning of the same week. The woman had been getting coffee. She had nodded at Kate in the way two women nodded at each other at six in the morning at a gas station. It was a face from a third place Kate could not put, on the same trip, in the same week, two and a half years ago.

Kate did not have the face's name.

She did not have the face's name yet.

She would. The name would not be a name Kate had heard before. The name would be a name Kate had been adjacent to without knowing it, the way a closure-eve survey was adjacent to all the lives an institution had touched without ever entering them. Today the face had no name. Today the face had a half pound of pepper turkey and a nod at a gas station and many months of being already-dead in a wall.

Owens stepped back from the cut. She had her phone in her hand. She had not taken it out; it had been in her hand. She dialed.

"Park," she said. "Renata. We have a homicide. Female, late thirties, Marston Hill State Hospital, second cavity East Wing partition between Ward 2-D and Ward 2-E. The body is fresh. I need you here in ninety minutes."

She listened.

"Tell them now."

She listened.

"Yes. The site is sealed."

She hung up.

"Welton."

"Yes."

"I'm sorry, this was not the find I told you we were going to make today. This is a different find."

"Yes."

"You are going to be at the start of the chain of custody on this case. The chain of custody on the cut order is on my paper as well as yours. You marked the partition on Day 3. You filed the order on Day 6. I personally signed off on the integrity of the chamber at one fifty-one this afternoon. All of that is documented."

"Okay."

Owens went back to the cut and began the next set of measurements. Hector took stills. Kate stood in the corridor with Ray. The cut crew was silent and the corridor lights were on full.

State police arrived at six oh nine. The lead detective introduced himself as James Park. Park was forty-seven, the registry call sheet had said forty-seven. He was lean and slow-moving and had a face that did not give away what it had been told. He took Kate's hand for the count of two and let it go.

"Welton."

"Park."

"You were the architect on the cut."

"I was."

"Walk me through it."

She walked him through it. He took notes by hand. He did not interrupt. He asked one question at the end, which was whether Kate had any reason to believe the cut crew or anyone on her contract had had access to the second cavity prior to the cut, which she said she did not. He nodded.

"More questions later. For now: who else has been on this site since you started."

"Ray Mendez. His foreman Doug. The cutter Marcus. The cut foreman Bill Voss and his two-man crew this morning. Eleanor Ross's granddaughter Tessa, by phone, not on-site. Wendell Kessler, twice on the perimeter and once at the trailer. Owens and Hector and the technicians. State troopers as of six tonight."

"Wendell Kessler."

"Yes."

"Twice on the perimeter and once at the trailer. Day 2 he came to the gate. Day 4 he came after Owens left from the basement find. He offered me access to his father's records at his house."

"Did you go."

"No."

"Smart."

"Yes."

By seven the demolition contractor had been on the phone with the state for an hour. The state wanted the building down on schedule. The demolition contract was non-refundable. The wreckers would start staging the morning of Day 9 for the originally scheduled Day 14 start, which was now a likely Day 14 start with a homicide investigation overlay. The east wing's second floor where the partition stood would be lifted and removed under tarp for evidentiary preservation. The rest of the demolition would proceed.

The state did not confirm this decision with Park in writing. The state called Park on the phone. Park said the call had been made. He did not say he agreed with it.

Kate, who had not been consulted, sent an email at seven nineteen to her editor at the Journal of American Historical Preservation and to the state preservation registry, copying Park, putting on the record that, in her professional opinion, the building should not come down until the homicide investigation was complete. She noted that her opinion had not been asked but had been entered for the file. She did not expect a reply.

She gave a four-hour statement to Park's officer at the trailer. She drank water she did not taste. She ate a granola bar she did not taste. She did not call her mother. She did not call her sister. She did not call Tessa Ross. She gave the statement in the order it had happened, with the times marked, on a fresh page of the field notebook a copy of which Park's officer photocopied page by page on the trailer's small printer.

Park came back at nine forty.

"Welton."

"Park."

"The body in the second cavity is being processed in place under tarp tonight. The body in the chair has been transported to the state lab in Owens's vehicle. The cordon is being expanded to include the entire east wing's second and third floors. State troopers are on the gate through the night. You will not be in the east wing tomorrow. You will be at the trailer. You will be available at all times. You will not leave the county without telling me."

"Okay."

"You did your job."

"Yes."

"You did it in a way that gave us an evidentiary chain. The chamber was intact. The cut was on the order. The forensic team was on-site within four hours of the find. The chain is good."

"Yes."

"That is not nothing."

"I know."

"Drive safe, Welton."

"Park." A small nod

She drove south.

The forty-one miles were the same ones she had driven seven times now and the rain had started again at mile marker sixteen. She did not turn the radio on. The wipers on the Outback failed at a stop sign and started again at the next one. The motel's vacancy sign was the orange of a forgotten porch light. Lori was at the desk with another paperback the size of a brick. Lori looked up.

"Long one."

"Long one."

"You eat?"

"No."

"There is a microwave thing in the freezer behind the desk. State troopers leave them for the locals on bad-weather nights. You can have one."

"Thank you."

"Welton."

"Lori."

"State troopers were at the gate up there an hour ago. Three cars."

"Yes."

"Anything I should know."

"Read the paper tomorrow."

She ate the food in Room 14 with the heater on. The lap blanket was over her knees, the laptop closed, the field notebook and the phone face down on the kitchenette table.

She did not call her mother or Joanne.

She sat on the edge of the bed in Room 14 and looked at the closed door and the closed curtains and the closed laptop and the closed notebook and the face-down phone, and she let what had happened be a thing that had happened without trying to control her feelings. She felt it and did not resist it.

Filing it away was tomorrow's job.

The midpoint of the contract had passed. The midpoint of any closure-eve survey had a certain quality. The building had given Kate what it was going to give her, and the rest of the contract was the work of documenting what she had. The midpoint of this contract had given her a hundred-year-old body in a chair and a body in a wall that was not a hundred years old. The asylum had been used. The use had not stopped at closure.

Whoever had used it had used it in the years since closure, the years the building had stood empty on the state's books and the wreckers had not yet come. Whoever had used it had been on the property in the months Park's missing-persons report would, on Day 10, put at eleven. Whoever had used it had been on the property recently enough that the second cavity's plaster had not yet cured at the seam.

ARCHIVE EXCERPT

Daily Eagle · May 14, 1994 · clipping found in admin filing cabinet

Dr. Kessler, left, with his son Wendell, recently licensed and joining a local practice, at the front gates. Photo by Sandra Dell.

MARSTON HILL STATE HOSPITAL TO CLOSE AFTER 121 YEARS

Final 84 patients to be transferred by August. Medical Director Dr. Theodore Kessler oversees the closure: "A difficult chapter ends. We will see that every patient is properly placed."

CHAPTER ELEVEN

A hospital three states away

Day 9 · morning

"Memory is the sense of loss, and loss pulls us after it."
— Marilynne Robinson, *Housekeeping* (1980)

Kate had slept four hours in Room 14. The heater had been set to 72 with the curtains closed and the alarm set for five. The alarm went off at five.

The drive back was forty-one miles in pre-dawn rain that stopped at the county line. The gate at Marston Hill was open at six fourteen because two state troopers were already there.

The senior trooper was Beasley according to his name badge. He was sixty and patient. The junior was Jensen, who was twenty-five and not yet patient. They had her credentials. They had her contract. They had Park's instructions on a printed sheet. The east wing was closed to Kate. The trailer and the central administration and the gravel lot were not. She thanked them. They nodded. She went to the field office.

The field office at six twenty-two was sixty-one degrees. She turned the heated vest up to medium, set the camp chair square against the wall under the south window, and laid her field bag at her feet.

She had work to do on Day 9 that did not involve the east wing, and Park had agreed to it the night before because her contract was binding and the state's preservation registry expected the contract delivered.

She did not start right away.

She sat in the camp chair and did not open the field notebook. The rain on the slate had started again and was slow and intermittent. She sat in the field office and listened to the slate.

The phone in her jacket pocket rang at seven fourteen.

Joanne.

She took it out. She answered on the first ring.

"Joanne."

"Kate."

A pause that wasn't a pause.

"Mom wandered."

She sighed, "When?"

"Last night. Police picked her up at the BP off Route 22 at four in the morning. Two coats. No shoes. They had to call the residence to find out where she belonged. The residence had a missing-persons protocol on her. They had not started it because the night staff had not done bed checks at the right interval, which is its own conversation."

"Yes."

"She was asking for Lila. She told the officer Lila was waiting for her at home and she needed to get there. She got the kitchen door open. She walked four miles."

"Four miles."

"On the shoulder of a state road in the rain in November. Without shoes."

"Not great."

"The hospital has her. Observation, fluids, monitoring overnight. They will keep her tonight and most of tomorrow. After that the residence has agreed to move her to the secure wing. The secure wing is what we have been talking about for six weeks."

"Okay."

"Kate."

A pause.

"Kate. Come now."

She did the math on driving time. It was five hours and change with traffic, six with stops. There was a flight to Albany at four ten that would not get her on the ground in time to be useful. There was no flight that would put her there before a drive. There was nothing west of the Berkshires today.

"Joanne."

"Kate."

"Listen."

"Kate."

"There is a body in a wall here. It was discovered in a wall yesterday. I gave a four-hour statement to the state police last night that ended at ten. The site is still under cordon. I'm the only person allowed on site who knows the building. The wreckers are scheduled for the tenth. The body that came out yesterday came out under my survey order. The chain of evidence runs through me. If I leave today, the chain has a hole in it on Day 9. Park won't get the case he is going to need."

"Kate."

"My contract ends on the tenth. I'll drive on the eleventh. I'll be there in the late evening. I'll be there for the move to the secure wing if the move is after the eleventh. If it has to happen before the eleventh, you and the residence can do it without me, and I'm sorry, but I am not coming today."

There was a silence on the line that was heavy. It was the silence of a hospital administrator on her way to the third coffee of a long day, and the third coffee was not going to help, and she knew it, and she was on the call anyway.

"Kate."

"I love you, Joanne."

"I love you too."

"I'm not coming today."

"I heard you."

"I'll come on the eleventh."

"On the eleventh."

"I will."

"And if she goes downhill."

"I'll come."

"You will."

"Yes."

She hung up.

She sat in the camp chair with the phone in her hand and looked out the south window at the meadow. The meadow had three hours of November sun on it now and the chicory was up and the dock was up and a single crow was crossing the meadow at a long diagonal that was the same long diagonal a crow had crossed the meadow on Day 1. A different crow.

She set the phone face down on the table.

She took the field notebook out of the side pocket. She opened it to the first blank page after the morning's notation, which was nothing, because she had not made a notation that morning. She put the pencil on the page.

The pencil did not move.

She looked at the page. She looked at the pencil. She looked at the page. The pencil sat on a blank page in a Field Notes notebook and did not move.

After five minutes she wrote.

She made a list of every architectural and documentary item she still had to verify before the wreckers' Friday cut, in the order she would do them. She wrote it in pencil and she did not look at her hand while she wrote it. Her hand was shaking. She did not look. The list was numbered. Each item had a verify-by date. Each verify-by date was on or before the thirteenth, because the wreckers had moved up to Friday from Monday after the Day 8 find and the buffer was now twenty-four hours. The list was forty-one items long.

The list was complete.

She closed the notebook.

She set the pencil down on the table beside the closed notebook.

Her hand was still shaking.

She put the heels of her palms over her eyes for a count of twenty, did not cry, took her hands down, and stood up.

The work for the day was the basement. The basement was not in the east wing. The basement was the hydrotherapy basement at the south end of the central administration's lower level,. It was within the cordon but Park had said yesterday she could enter with a state trooper present. She had asked for Beasley. Park had said yes. Beasley would be on the basement door at fourteen hundred.

Until fourteen hundred she had four hours.

She crossed the rear corridor to the records room.

The records room was still twenty by twenty-four with a plaster ceiling and four walls of cabinets, and on Day 5 in the storm she had inventoried the four drawers in the cabinet by the door. They had been empty except for a single brass paperclip and a 1924 intake form for Pemberton, Alice Margaret, which had been in the wrong drawer and which had not been there twenty minutes later. She had photographed it twice. She had given the photographs to Park. The form had appeared on the chapel altar on Day 7 and disappeared again forty-six minutes after she found it. The form was at present in two cloud accounts and not in any drawer at Marston Hill State Hospital.

She had four cabinets left.

She put on the gloves. She set the headlamp to medium. She started at the top drawer of the cabinet against the east wall.

ADMISSIONS 1947 to 1952. Empty.

ADMISSIONS 1953 to 1958. Empty.

ADMISSIONS 1959 to 1964. Empty.

ADMISSIONS 1965 to 1968. Empty.

She moved to the cabinet beside it.

DISCHARGE 1929 to 1934. Empty.

DISCHARGE 1935 to 1940. Empty.

DISCHARGE 1941 to 1946. Empty.

DISCHARGE 1947 to 1952. Empty, with a brittle hairpin against the back panel that she did not remove and that she logged in the field notebook.

She moved to the third cabinet.

The third cabinet was the cabinet she had been ignoring since Day 5, on the south wall, the one labeled

INTAKE/DISCHARGE 1990 to 1994. This cabinet she had been ignoring because it was the closure-era cabinet, and the closure-era records were the records that overlapped Wendell's intern year and Theo's last five years as medical director. Kate had not been ready to know what was and was not in those drawers.

She was ready now.

She pulled the drawer.

The drawer slid easily on its rollers, as though it had been pulled all the way out and shoved back many times in the past month.

The drawer was full.

The drawer was full of folders, in date order, color-tabbed by year. Closure-era. Intact.

Kate, in the records room of the central administration of Marston Hill State Hospital on Day 9 of a fourteen-day contract, with her mother in observation three states south and a body in a wall under tarp on the second floor of the east wing thirty feet from her, looked at the closure-era folders in the closure-era drawer. The folders were the only folders she had found in any drawer in this room. They had been put in the drawer. The folders had been put in the drawer recently.

She did not, for the count of ten, touch them.

She wrote in the notebook:

Records room, Cabinet 3 (south wall), top drawer (INTAKE/DISCHARGE 1990–1994): drawer is full. Folders intact, color-tabbed, date order. Drawer slides freely on rollers, suggesting recent use. Discovered 09:48 Day 9. Did not open folders. Photographing in place before any handling.

She closed the notebook.

She raised the Pentax. She took eight stills of the closed drawer and four of the folder spines visible from above. She set the camera down. She put a strip of blue tape on the front of the cabinet at the level of the top drawer and wrote the time and her initials on the tape with the pencil. She closed the drawer.

She was going to call Park before she opened a folder.

She left the records room and went back to the field office and called Park.

Park picked up on the second ring.

"Welton."

"Park."

"Tell me."

She told him. He took it down. He said he would have a forensic doc tech on-site by noon. She said thank you and hung up.

She sat at the table under the south window. The meadow was still there. The crow had not come back.

Margaret was in a hospital in Connecticut. Margaret was, by the math, two hundred and eighty miles south by interstate, and Kate was not going.

Kate put the heels of her palms over her eyes a second time but still did not cry. She took her hands down. The work for the morning had changed. The work for the morning was now waiting for the forensic doc tech and writing down what she had not opened.

She did the work.

CHAPTER TWELVE

Kate does not leave

Day 9 · evening into night

"When you are in the middle of a story it isn't a story at all, but only a confusion; a dark roaring, a blindness."

— Margaret Atwood, *Alias Grace* (1996)

The forensic document technician was a woman named Pham who had a master's degree in archival science, a state badge, and the kind of unhurried way of opening a file folder Kate had only ever seen in archivists. She arrived at eleven forty. She processed the closure-era drawer in the records room across the corridor from Kate's field office for three hours, photographing each folder before she opened it, and at three oh four she came across the corridor and put a hand on the door of the field office.

"Welton. The drawer is yours."

"Thanks."

"You can sit with the drawer. You cannot remove anything from the drawer. Anything you want to read, you read in the room. Anything you want to copy, I copy. You are on the chain of custody as of two thirty."

"Okay."

"I'm going to be in the trailer for the next four hours doing the paperwork on what I just photographed. I will check on you at five and at seven. After seven you have the room until I come back at eight tomorrow morning. The state troopers are on the gate."

"Thank you."

She left.

Kate went into the records room with the laptop and a thermos of water and the lap blanket and the field notebook and a sharpened pencil. Beasley was at the corridor's south end with a chair from the trailer, reading a paperback, and he did not look up when she went past. She had already postponed the basement work to a later date,

The closure-era drawer had ninety-two folders in it. The folders were tabbed by year and within year by surname. The records covered intake and discharge from January 1990 through August 1994. Eighty-eight folders contained patient files corresponding to patients who appeared in the federal census submissions of those years, in the state archive's surviving record, and in the institutional ledger of the on-grounds cemetery. Those eighty-eight reconciled.

Four did not.

The four sat on the chair beside her at five fourteen, after she had pulled them from the date order and stacked them. Each folder was a discharge and each discharge was a transfer to a receiving institution. Each receiving institution, on the laptop running searches against the state's licensed-facility registry, did not exist on the date of the transfer.

The first transfer was 1992 to St. Catherine's Home for the Convalescent in Springfield, which had closed in 1989.

The second was 1993 to a private group home in Pittsfield with a license number that returned no result in the state registry.

The third was 1994 to a state hospital in New Hampshire that had taken state-transferred patients only from upstate New York, not from this state, and which had no record of the patient on file when Kate ran the patient name through the lookup the duty archivist had given her access to on Day 4.

Three women. None of them at the institution they were supposed to be at. None of them known to be alive on the public record after the year of the transfer. None of them with a death certificate filed in any of the three states the receiving facilities had been in.

Kate wrote in the field notebook:

Records room, closure-era drawer: 92 folders. 88 reconcile to state archive, federal census, on-grounds cemetery ledger. 4 do not. Discharges in 1992, 1993, 1994, 2024; receiving institutions either closed before transfer date, or do not exist in state registry, or have no record of receipt. Women's names withheld in this entry until I have crossed them against the missing-persons rolls. Cross-check 18:00 tomorrow with Park.

She closed the notebook.

She did not call Park yet. She had work that came first.

The state archive dossier on her laptop was 1924 to 1940. The dossier was not the dossier she had asked for; she had asked for admissions and discharge records for 1924 to 1940 because she already had the records from 1941 to 1994. The archivist had pulled what survived, which was admissions intact for that span and discharges in fragments. The fragments were what the archivist had been able to pull in three days. There was more in the capital. She had asked for it on the morning of Day 6 with no return date.

She opened the fragments.

She had read them once on Day 7 before she went to the chapel and was still reading them now. She had previously read them as background. She compared them now to the on-grounds cemetery ledger, which the registry call sheet had told her was maintained on a 1971 IBM Selectric carbon ledger that survived in the basement of the regional historical society in town and which had been digitized in 2017 by a local volunteer with a flatbed scanner and very good lighting.

She had the digital scan of the cemetery ledger on the laptop.

She had had it since Day 1.

She had not, until tonight, needed it.

She ran through it now. She ran it against the discharge fragments. She ran it against the intake fragments. She ran it against the state archive's surviving incident reports. She ran it against the federal census submissions of 1930, 1940, and 1950.

It took her four hours.

At nine fourteen she had the gap.

The gap was forty-seven women.

Forty-seven discharges between 1923 and 1962, marked in the surviving record as *transferred — destination unrecorded*, with no corresponding receiving institution and no death certificate filed in any state and no entry in the on-grounds cemetery ledger.

Forty-seven women who left the institution on paper and did not arrive anywhere on paper and were not buried on paper.

Forty-seven plus four. The four from the closure-era drawer.

Fifty-one.

She wrote in the field notebook:

1923 to 1962: 47 discharges marked "transferred — destination unrecorded," no receiving institution, no DC, no on-grounds cemetery entry. 1990 to 1994: 3 discharges with similar pattern. 2024: 1 discharge. Total: 50 women unaccounted for in 71 years of the institution's operation. Once since closure. Pattern persistent across regimes; intensifies in closure era.

She closed the notebook and sat still.

She got up. She walked to where the south window of the records room would have been if the records room had a window. She walked back to the chair. She sat in the chair. She put the heels of her palms over her eyes. She took her hands down.

The most recent of the three closure-era discharges was 1994. There was a fourth.

The fourth was after closure.

The fourth was Beth Carrow.

Kate had noted Beth Carrow on Day 4, when Wendell Kessler had introduced himself at the trailer step. The registry call sheet had Wendell Kessler's father's name as the deceased head of the hospital contact and had Beth Carrow's mother's name as the last administrator. She had not noticed the connection at the time. The connection had been a name on a sheet.

It was no longer a name on a sheet.

She opened the laptop. She pulled up the state's missing-persons database. She entered Beth Carrow.

The entry was current. Beth Carrow, age thirty-eight when last seen, missing eleven months, last known address in town, missing-persons report filed by mother Catherine Carrow on June 14 of the prior year, no leads.

Beth Carrow had been a reporter at the regional weekly paper and a paralegal before that. Beth Carrow had spent a weekend at the records storage of Marston Hill State Hospital in 2023 with the permission of her mother, the last administrator. Beth Carrow, in the missing-persons report, had been at work on a regional history piece about asylum closures in the Northeast. Her mother had thought it was a regional history piece. Her mother had been wrong about a great many things, by the look of the missing-persons report.

Kate ran a search against the state's licensed-facility registry for the receiving institution listed on the May 2024 forged discharge document Pham had photographed and given her digital access to at three eleven that afternoon. The discharge listed Beth Carrow as transferred to a private behavioral-health facility in the next county over, with a license number.

The license number returned no result.

The signature on the discharge was not Catherine Carrow's signature. Kate had two of Catherine Carrow's signatures from the 1992 and 1993 discharges in the closure-era drawer and a third from the 1994 closure press materials in the historical society's online holdings. The signature on Beth Carrow's discharge was a person's attempt at Catherine Carrow's signature done from memory rather than from a sample, by someone who had seen Catherine Carrow sign a thing once and who had not photographed the signature before they tried it.

The forgery had not had to be great. Beth had been the last administrator's daughter, and the forgery was on a closure-era institution that had been closed for thirty years. The institution would be coming down on Friday, and the forgery had only needed to survive the eleven months between Beth's disappearance and the demolition.

It had survived eleven of those months.

Kate had broken it on the twelfth.

She wrote in the field notebook:

Beth Carrow, age 39 at present, missing 11 months. Forged discharge dated May 2024, signature inauthentic vs. Catherine Carrow exemplars from 1992–1994 closure-era drawer + 1994 press materials. Receiving facility license no. invalid. Beth was researching regional asylum closures. Beth had access to records storage in 2023. Beth's mother was last administrator. Cross-ref. Day 8 second-cavity body to missing-persons photo at first opportunity.

She did not write the name on the second-cavity body.

She did not write the name because Owens had not identified the body yet. The survey supervisor was not the person to write a name on a body that had not been identified by the people whose job it was to identify it.

The survey supervisor was, however, allowed to know.

The survey supervisor knew.

She closed the notebook.

For a moment, she allowed the knowledge to be a thing she was holding rather than a thing she had written down.

She finally noted it.

She did not call Joanne. She did not call Tessa Ross. She did not call Margaret. She called Park.

Park picked up on the second ring.

“Welton.”

“Park.”

“Tell me.”

She told him. She told him in the order of the work, which was the way she told things to people who took notes by hand: the gap of forty-seven, the three closure-era discharges, the forged 2024 signature line, the closure-era pattern, the post-closure repetition, the name she had crossed and not written. He listened. He took notes. He did not interrupt.

When she had finished he said:

“Welton.”

“Yes.”

“We need to have a different conversation in seventy-two hours.”

“Okay.”

“I’m going to need everything you have walked me through, on paper, on the chain of custody. I’m going to need a forensic doc tech to cross-stamp it. I’ll have Pham do that tomorrow. You are going to come into the station tomorrow afternoon to give a second statement. The statement will be on the cross-checks against the on-grounds cemetery ledger and the missing-persons database. Three hours, with breaks.”

“I’ll be there.”

“Welton.”

“Yes.”

“You did this work in nine hours from a standing start. You found a gap that wasn’t visible from the discharge fragments alone.”

“I had the cemetery ledger. I had the state archive. I had a closure-era drawer.”

A pause.

"Welton?"

"Yes."

"I'm going to ask the state police evidence unit to go to the Kessler house tomorrow morning at six and pull the records he has in his dining room, on a warrant. The warrant is being drafted tonight. I'll have it before nine."

"Alright."

"You're not going to the Kessler house."

"No."

"Drive safe to the motel, Welton."

"I'm at the trailer tonight."

"You are not."

"Park."

"Drive south."

She did not answer for the count of three.

"Fine."

"Welton."

"Yes."

"I'm the lead investigator on a homicide that runs through the architecture of the building you are sitting in. I'm not going to have a survey supervisor sleep there. Drive south."

"Okay, okay, I'll drive south."

"Okay."

She hung up.

She closed the laptop. She put the gloves in the bag. She put the field notebook in the side pocket. She drank the rest of the water. She turned off the headlamp. She left the records room.

Beasley was at the chair at the south end of the corridor. He looked up.

"Long one," he said.

"Long one."

"You eat."

"Granola bar."

"There is a microwave thing in the trailer. I'll heat it for you while you load the car."

Beasley nodded to her and went to heat the microwave meal.

Kate walked out the front door of the central administration and across the gravel to the Outback. The November sky was inky black darkness by ten and the wind off the meadow was up. The wreckers' equipment in the gravel lot was in the same configuration it had been in on Day 8, tarped against the wind that was not yet a storm. The trailer light was on. Beasley was inside.

She loaded the field bag and the laptop case. She did not put the keys in the ignition. She stood beside the open driver's-side door and looked at Marston Hill the way she had looked at it for nine days now. She hoped it was a building with little left to give.

The chapel-corridor between the central administration and the detached chapel held its forty-six. She could not see it from where she stood. It held its forty-six anyway.

The east wing's second-floor partition between Ward 2-D and Ward 2-E, where on Day 8 the chamber had given up a hundred-year-old woman in a chair and the cavity behind the chair had given up Beth Carrow, was tarped now and would, on Friday, be on a flatbed.

Kate Margaret Welton was thirty-eight, and four years older than Beth Carrow had ever gotten to be.

She got in the Outback. She turned the key. The dashboard glowed: clock, fuel gauge, the field thermometer read thirty-nine outside and sixty inside. Beasley came out of the trailer with a foil pan and a paper towel. She rolled the window down. She took it and thanked him. He nodded.

She drove south.

CHAPTER THIRTEEN

Beth Carrow

Day 10

"You won't know — till afterwards. It's only afterwards that you know."
— Edith Wharton, *Afterward* (1910)

Park called at five forty-three.

She had been awake since five. The motel room at the Cedarwood was sixty-eight by the thermostat and quiet. She had made a cup of instant coffee at five fifteen and was sitting at the kitchenette table with the laptop open to the Day 9 notebook entries when the phone rang.

"Welton."

"Park."

"Eight at the station. Bring the field notebook and the laptop. Bring the print of the Beth Carrow missing-persons photograph from the database."

"I have it."

"And the discharge document."

"Pham has the original. I have a verified copy."

"Bring it."

"Will do."

"Welton."

"Yes."

"I'm not going to allow you back on-site today. You will be at the station this morning and I want you to stay in town the rest of the day. The state evidence unit is at the Kessler house starting at six. The Marston

Hill site is closed to you and the contractor and anyone but the troopers and the forensic team until I open it again."

"Okay."

"The people who write the next eight days of the news are going to want to ask you questions. I'll keep you out of their reach."

"Thank you."

"Drive safe."

"Yes."

She hung up.

She drank the rest of the coffee. She showered. She put on the second of the three field-clothing sets she had packed for the contract, which was the set she put on when she expected to be photographed and did not want to be remembered for the photograph. Charcoal canvas pants. Charcoal long-sleeve. Charcoal field jacket. The boots were the same boots as always.

She drove into town at seven oh four.

The town was quiet. The diner that was now an LLC operating under a name in a font nobody had bought since 1991, was open and had three trucks in the lot. The historical society wasn't open yet. The medical board's office on Howard Street had a single light on in the back. She did not slow at the medical board's office. She drove past it the way she had driven past it on the morning of Day 6, when she had gone to bring Eleanor Ross yellow flowers, and she did not look in.

Park's station was at the south edge of town in a low brick building from 1971 that had been the post office before it was the police station and was now both, with the post office in the front half and the state police in the back. She parked behind the building. Park was at the back door with a coffee.

"Welton."

"Park."

She went inside.

Park's interview room was eight by ten. There was a metal table and two metal chairs and a fluorescent panel overhead that flickered at the south end. The room had one window with the blind drawn. There was a folder on the table.

The folder was the missing-persons file on Beth Carrow.

"Sit down."

She sat.

He sat across from her.

"I'm going to walk you through the protocol on a preliminary visual identification. The protocol is that a person who has had visual contact with the missing person in life can review a photograph of the recovered body and confirm or deny that the recovered body matches the missing person they recall. The protocol is preliminary. It does not stand up in court. It is what we do to know whether to call the family before the dental records come back."

"Okay."

"You saw Beth Carrow on three occasions in the spring of 2024, on your pre-survey trip to this town. You did not know her name. You stated to me on Day 8 that she nodded at you at the gas station and was in line in front of you at the deli at the supermarket and was at a third location you cannot place."

"Yes."

"I'm going to show you a photograph. I'm going to ask you whether the person in the photograph is the same person you saw on those three occasions. You will take as long as you need to answer."

He opened the folder.

There was a four-by-six color print. The photograph was of a woman who was thirty-eight or thereabouts, sitting at a kitchen table with a coffee cup in her hand, looking sideways at the camera as though she had not asked to be photographed. It had been taken at a family event by someone who had not been Beth Carrow's mother and had been provided to the missing-persons report by Catherine Carrow on June 14 of the prior year.

Kate looked at the photograph.

The face was the face from the deli counter. The face was the face from the gas station. The face was the face from the third place she could not put, on the same trip, in the same week, two and a half years ago.

"That is the woman."

"You're sure?"

"I'm sure."

"You're sure how."

"I have a memory for faces I have noted in the field. I noted this face three times in one week without knowing a name. That is the nod from the gas station and the half-pound of pepper turkey at the deli. That is the face Owens cut out of a wall on Day 8."

"Makes sense."

"Park."

"Yes."

"I'm sorry."

"You are not the person I need an apology from."

He closed the folder.

"This is preliminary. Catherine Carrow will be brought in for the formal identification this afternoon. She will be in this room at three. I won't need you for that. You will not be in the building for that."

"I'm not family."

"Right, you are the witness who found the body."

"Right."

He took the folder off the table. He set it on the chair beside him.

"Welton."

"Yes."

"First, you did the work of an investigator yesterday. Second, that the work of an investigator is not the work the state contracted you for, and it is not the work the press is going to recognize you for. The press is going to write that the survey supervisor on the building closure found a body and that the state forensic anthropologist identified it. The press is not going to write that you cross-checked a discharge gap of fifty women across seventy-one years in nine hours. But I know."

"Thank you."

"The chain of custody on what you did yesterday will hold. Pham has it. I have it. The state archive has it. When it goes in front of an attorney it will be a chain that runs through three professionals. You shouldn't have to testify, that will be me. But we may need one affidavit."

"Sure."

He stood up. He walked to the door. He opened the door.

"Go out the back. Stay in town today. There is a coffee shop on Main called the Beech. There is a public library two blocks east of it that has the historical society's microfilm in the basement. You can spend the day there. I'll have a trooper at the gate of Marston Hill until I tell you otherwise. The contractor and the wreckers are on hold. Ray is at home. If you need to call me, call. If I need you, I'll call."

"Okay."

She went out the back.

The day in town was long. She had a coffee at the Beech and read a paperback she had bought at the gas station off Route 8 the week before and could not remember the plot of. She had lunch at the diner that was now an LLC operating under a name in a font nobody had bought since 1991. She walked the historical society's microfilm of the *Daily Eagle* from 1990 to 1994 in the library basement and noted three articles about closure-era Marston Hill she had not seen on the digital index. She copied them. She put on the cotton gloves the librarian gave her and did not take them off until the librarian closed at four.

The phone rang at four eleven.

It was Park.

"Welton."

"Park. Beasley just called from the gate. There is a charcoal Audi in the lot. The man got out ten minutes ago, walked up the steps of the central administration, and is sitting on the portico with a thermos. Beasley wants to know whose car it is."

"It is Wendell Kessler's."

"You're sure."

"Charcoal Audi, four years old, washed within the week. I photographed it on Day 4 at the trailer."

"I'm sending two from the station. Eleven minutes."

"Where do you want me."

"You can stay where you are. The two will handle it. I called you because if it is his car I want it confirmed at distance."

"I'm twelve minutes from the gate."

"You don't have to go."

"I know."

"If you go, do not get out of the vehicle. Park ten yards behind the equipment line. See what's in the lot. You can confirm the car. Wait for my two to arrive. Do not engage with Kessler. Do not exit the vehicle for any reason. Beasley has been told."

"Good."

"Welton."

"Yes."

"You don't have to go."

"I'm going."

She hung up.

She got in the Outback.

She drove back to Marston Hill at sunset.

The November sky at sunset was the color of the inside of a shell. The leaves on the maples along the access road had gone past color and were the brown of leaves too long on the branch. The walnut crowns ahead of the access road were bare.

She slowed at the bend in the access road where the building came clear through the trees.

The wreckers' equipment was no longer staged in the gravel lot.

Instead, it was staged on the access road, twenty yards inside the gate, lined up in the order it would be deployed on the morning of November tenth. Two excavators. A dozer. A skid steer with an attachment crane. The grapple. The water truck. The cone perimeter had been moved out to the equipment line. The trooper on the gate raised a hand as she came up. She raised hers. He waved her through.

She came around to the gravel lot.

Wendell Kessler's car was in the gravel lot.

The car was a charcoal Audi, four years old, washed within the week. It was parked beside Ray's foreman's truck, which was empty. Ray's foreman's truck had been at the site on Day 8 and had stayed. The trooper had let it stay because he was not told to move it.

Wendell Kessler was on the four shallow steps of the portico of the central administration.

He had a thermos. The thermos was the stainless Stanley with the worn blue grip Kate had photographed on Day 4 at the trailer after the morgue find and had filed against the dossier she would later turn over to Park. He had a coffee in a separate paper cup, half-drunk, on the step beside him. He had a barn coat, the same barn coat from Day 2 at the gate. He had no hat.

He stood up when she pulled into the lot. He did not come down.

She did not get out of the car.

She picked up the phone. She called Park.

Park picked up on the first ring.

"Welton."

"Park. Wendell Kessler is on the portico of the central administration."

A pause.

"How long."

"I don't know how long. He stood up when I pulled in."

"Stay in the car. Lock the doors. Do not turn the engine off. Two troopers are on their way from the station now. They will be there in nine minutes. Is the gate trooper visible?"

"At the gate."

"Tell him on the radio. The contractor radio is the band you and he can both use."

"Yes."

"Welton?"

"Yes."

"He is not going to do anything to you on the portico. He came because he wanted you to know he can. Do not get out of the car."

"I'm not getting out of the car."

"Nine minutes."

She hung up.

She did not turn the engine off. She did not unlock the doors. She put the car in park. She put her hands at ten and two on the wheel because the wheel was a thing to put her hands on. The engine idled. The dashboard glowed.

Wendell Kessler stood on the top of the four shallow steps of the portico of the 1873 central administration of Marston Hill State Hospital, drinking a coffee from a paper cup he had brought from town.

He did not move, he did not smile, and he did not look away.

The chapel-corridor between the central administration and the detached chapel held its forty-six. She could not see it from where she was. It held its forty-six anyway.

The two troopers came up the access road at six oh nine. She saw their headlights in the rearview before she heard the engines. They cleared the gate and parked behind her in the gravel. They got out and walked past her. They walked to the foot of the four shallow steps of the portico. They asked Wendell Kessler to come down. He came down. They asked him for identification. He provided it. They asked him to come with them to the station for a conversation with Detective Park. He agreed.

He walked past her car as they led him to one of their two vehicles. He did not look at her car.

He left a small white square on the third step of the portico when he stood up. The small white square was a folded paper napkin from the Beech, the coffee shop on Main where she had spent the morning. The napkin was folded into quarters. The napkin had not been there before he sat on the step.

She did not get out of the car for that, either.

She called Park.

"Park."

"He left a napkin on the step of the portico."

"Don't touch it."

"I'm not touching it."

"Send the trooper for it. I'll have a tech process it tonight."

"Good."

"Welton?"
"Yes."
"You should not be on site tonight either."
"Okay."
"Drive south."
"I'm driving south."
She hung up.
She drove south.

ARCHIVE EXCERPT

Marston Hill State Hospital · Internal Incident Report · March 12, 1989

MARSTON HILL

No follow-up form attached. Patient does not appear in Q2 census.

INCIDENT REPORT

DATE: March 12, 1989

PATIENT: Sandra K.

AGE: 23

SEX: F

transferred to Ward 4-E this date for behavioral deterioration following family visit.
Prior incidents: 0.
Recommendation: Increased oversight; clinical son W. Kessler (intern, second year) supervising overnight rotations through the duration.

FILED BY: T. Kessler
(DOCTOR)

WITNESSED BY: ______________________
(NURSING STAFF)

CHAPTER FOURTEEN

The building closes

Day 11

"Your silence will not protect you."

— Audre Lorde, *Sister Outsider* (1984)

She was at the gate at five fifty-seven.

The trooper on the gate was Beasley by the second night. Beasley had been on the gate from nine last night to six this morning. A twelve hour shift. He had three hours left before he was relieved. He wasn't feeling patient at hour nine of a twelve. He was patient anyway.

"Welton."

"Beasley."

"Park called. Said you might come."

"Yes."

"He said if you came early, he wasn't going to have me stop you. The police will be here at eight. Do not enter the cordoned floors. Do not enter the chamber. The basement door is yours if you want to use it. He said I am to be at the basement door at eight oh five regardless of where you are."

"Okay."

"He said one other thing."

"What."

"He said to tell you that the keys still work because the state contractor did not yet revoke them, and that the keys would be collected at eight today. This was not an instruction. It was a fact."

"Okay."

"He said you would understand."

"I do."

He raised the gate.

She drove through.

The gravel lot at six oh one was empty. The wreckers' equipment was on the access road behind her, where it had been on the evening of Day 10. The trailer was dark. Ray was not on-site. The cordon tape across the front door of the central administration had been cut by the state evidence team on Day 10 and re-taped with a fresh strip of yellow plastic that read CRIME SCENE DO NOT CROSS in black ink, lifted at one corner where someone had walked under it and not taped it back down.

She walked under the lifted corner. She did not retape it.

She had three hours.

She did a quick inventory. Field bag, field notebook, the Pentax, and the headlamp. She had the heated vest on high under the jacket. She had a thermos of black coffee from the Cedarwood front desk and a granola bar in the inside pocket and the second set of cotton gloves the librarian had given her on Day 10 in the library basement and not asked her to return.

She walked through the front door of the central administration at six oh three.

She went to the records room and unlocked the closure-era drawer with the key Pham had given her on Day 9. She did not open the drawer. She put a hand on the front of the drawer and stood there for a minute and then went to the stairs at the south end of the rear corridor.

The stairs to the lower level of the central administration were 1924 brick on an 1873 stone foundation. They went down at a thirty-degree pitch with a half-landing six steps down and a turn at the half-landing and six more steps down. The hydrotherapy basement was at the south end of the lower level, behind a steel door painted institutional green.

The steel door was unlocked.

She stood at the top of the lower flight and looked down at the steel door and the bolt on the outside of the steel door.

The bolt on the outside of the steel door was the bolt Eleanor Ross had told her about on Day 6 in her armchair at the assisted-living residence, in the tone of a woman who had told her granddaughter on a Tuesday morning to fetch a sweater.

She had three hours.

She went down the stairs.

The bolt on the door was open. The bolt was a piece of brass on a piece of steel that was on the outside of the door. The bolt was open. She pushe the door inward with the back of her gloved hand and stepped inside.

She did not close the door behind her.

The hydrotherapy basement at six fourteen on Day 11 was fifty-two degrees as measured by her tablet. The basement was lit by the overhead fluorescents she had turned on at the head of the stairs, which were old and yellow and which threw shadows across the corner of the room near the basin where the cabinet and the duty desk had been since 1924. The smell on the staircase down had been wet plaster and rat with a fungal note. The smell in the basement itself was the smell of the staircase, only fainter, with a cold layer on top that Kate understood as the smell a tile drain still had after thirty years of disuse.

The basement was four rooms.

The first was the cold-treatment room. Two long tubs, original 1924 cast iron, sheathed in tile that had been white in 1924 but now the color of an old bath in a closed institution. The tubs were full of folded canvas that was not historical. The canvas was dry. The canvas was stacked. The canvas had been put there recently.

She did not touch it.

The second was the shock-treatment room. The shock equipment had been dismantled in 1986 but not removed. The frame of the table was still bolted to the floor. The leather wrist and ankle straps had been cut from the frame and laid on the floor beside it, as though they had been removed by a person who intended to clean the room and had been interrupted. The straps were the same leather and the same buckles as the straps Owens had cut from the chair in the East Wing chamber on Day 8.

She did not touch the straps.

The third was the basin room. There was a wash basin with a tap that had been turned off at the riser in 1994. The tap was now back on at the riser. The basin had standing water in it the depth of a thumb. The water was cold when she measured it. The basin itself was sixty-one degrees. The basin had been used in the past forty-eight hours.

She did not touch the basin.

The fourth door led to the duty room. The duty room was nine by twelve with a single hanging light, no window, a wooden duty desk against the back wall, and behind the duty desk a recessed cabinet built into the brick. The recessed cabinet was the cabinet Eleanor Ross had told her about on Day 6.

The recessed cabinet had a lock. The lock was a Mosler five-pin, gone the color of old pennies at the keyway, the same Mosler five-pin as the lock on the basement door upstairs, which had been on Eleanor Ross's old key set.

The recessed cabinet was unlocked.

Inside the recessed cabinet was a steel file box.

The steel file box was the kind of file box a state hospital had bought by the gross in 1962 for medication-storage backup. The box was painted institutional green and had a hasp. The hasp was unlatched.

She lifted the lid of the box.

Inside the box were photographs.

The photographs were not historical. They were on standard four-by-six photo paper. The photographs had been printed within the last five years on a consumer-grade inkjet printer on paper that had not yet yellowed at the edges.

The photographs were of women.

The women in the top photographs were not in 1924 institutional dress. They were in the dress of women in the second decade of the twenty-first century. The women had not been told the photographs were being taken. They were posed. The women were in the beige and the white and the soft pastel of women who had been to a private practice for psychiatric care and had been, in the practice, made to undress beyond what the practice required. The women were drugged.

She turned over a photograph at the top of the stack.

The photograph at the top of the stack was of Beth Carrow, alive, sitting in a wing chair; the wing chair Wendell Kessler had at his private practice on Howard Street. Beth Carrow was wearing a hospital gown. She was looking sideways at the camera the way Beth Carrow had looked sideways at the camera in the photograph her mother had given the missing-persons report. Only in the missing-persons photograph Beth Carrow had been at a kitchen table and in this photograph she was in a wing chair on Howard Street with a hospital gown on her body and a needle mark in the crease of her left elbow.

She turned over the next photograph.

Sandra K. The photograph was older than the others. The photograph was of a woman in her early twenties in 1989 institutional dress. The handwriting on the back of the photograph, in pencil, was the same handwriting as the 1989 incident report on Sandra K. that Kate had read in the state archive dossier on Day 7. The handwriting was Theodore Kessler's.

The next photograph.

The next photograph.

The next.

There were forty-one photographs in the box. They spanned thirty-two years. The earliest was 1989. The most recent was Beth Carrow.

There were three more photographs taken after Beth Carrow.

She did not get to those.

She put the lid on the box. She took the box out of the recessed cabinet. She turned to leave the duty room.

The basement door at the head of the stairs had closed.

She moved across the duty room and through the basin room and through the shock-treatment room and through the cold-treatment room and to the foot of the stairs and up the stairs to the steel door at the top.

The steel door was closed. She put her gloved hand on the handle. She pulled.

The door did not move.

She put her shoulder against the door. She pushed. She heard, on the other side of the door, the small dry click of a brass bolt seating in a steel keep.

The bolt on the outside was closed.

She stood on the top step of the lower flight of the staircase to the lower level of the central administration of Marston Hill State Hospital, at six twenty-eight on the morning of November seventh, with a steel file box of forty-one photographs in her left hand, the field notebook in the side pocket of her field jacket, the Pentax around her neck, the headlamp on her forehead, the heated vest on high under the jacket, and the bolt closed on the outside of the door that was the only way out of the hydrotherapy basement of an asylum that had been closed for thirty-two years and was coming down on November tenth. She was alone.

The fluorescents at the head of the stairs went out.

The fluorescents at the foot of the stairs went out.

The fluorescents in the cold-treatment room went out.

The fluorescents in the shock-treatment room went out.

The fluorescent in the basin room went out.

The hanging light in the duty room went out.

The basement was dark.

She did not move.

CHAPTER FIFTEEN

Recognition

Day 12 · before dawn

"If life be a war, it seemed my destiny to conduct it single-handed."
— Charlotte Brontë, *Villette* (1853)

She froze for one minute.

The headlamp came on at six twenty-nine. The white circle on the steel door at the head of the stairs was the size of a dinner plate. The bolt on the outside of the door was, by the sound of the click she had heard at six twenty-eight, fully seated in the steel keep.

She set the file box on the top step. She took the field notebook from the side pocket and wrote:

Hydrotherapy basement, 06:30 Day 11. Locked in. Bolt on outside of upper door, seated. Lights cut at 06:28. Headlamp operational, full battery. Field bag with chisel, multitool, headlamp battery spare. Cellular signal: zero in the basement; intermittent on the upper landing. Will check at intervals. Will work the door.

She closed the notebook.

She lifted the file box off the top step and carried it down the lower flight of the staircase to the foot of the stairs. She set it on the floor of the cold-treatment room, against the base of the first cast-iron tub, where it was below the line a person standing in the doorway would see. She went back up the stairs.

She checked the phone. It had no signal at the foot of the stairs, no signal at the half-landing, and one bar at the top step.

She wrote a draft text to Park and saved it to the drafts folder but did not send it. She had no idea who was reading Park's messages and had no idea whether the bar at the top step was a real bar or a phantom. She pressed the side-key three times instead, which was the way the phone was set to dial Park automatically with a recording of any audio on the line. The call connected for the count of four. The call dropped.

The bar at the top step had been a phantom.

She put the phone in the inside pocket of her field jacket and went to work on the door.

The steel door was the kind a state hospital had bought by the gross in 1924 for plant rooms and basement entries: half-inch plate, double-hinged on the inside, dead-bolted on the outside. The hinges were on her side. The bolt was not. The hinges were the strap-pin type the 1924 plant catalogues had specified for a basement door that opened inward. The hinge pins were five-eighths brass. They had been in their straps since 1924 and had not been pulled in a hundred and two years.

She had a chisel.

She knelt on the top step. She set the field bag beside her and took the chisel out of it. The chisel was a one-inch flat from the field bag's tool roll, hardened steel, edge dressed by Kate herself in the Subaru's hatch on the morning of Day 1 because she expected to use it on a closure-eve survey and she did not begin a contract with a dull edge.

She put the chisel under the head of the upper hinge pin. She tapped the chisel butt with the heel of her hand.

The pin did not move.

She tapped again. Harder.

The pin moved by an eighth.

She tapped again.

By ten in the morning the upper hinge pin was out. It was three and three quarters of an inch long. She put the pin in the field bag.

At noon she ate the granola bar.

At one she heard, faintly, sound from the foyer above, which she guessed was feet on the floorboards and which she did not call out to. Calling out through a half-inch steel plate three meters of brick below the foyer was useless. By two the sound from above had stopped and she was working the lower hinge pin.

The lower hinge pin took the rest of the afternoon and the early hours of the evening. She broke for water at four and six. By eight in the evening she had two pins in the field bag and the door was held only by the bolt on the outside and by its own weight in the strap-tubes.

The door did not move.

The door did not move because it was a steel plate weighing approximately one hundred and twenty pounds, and it was wedged against the brick of the door frame with a hundred and two years of paint that had welded the hinge straps to the strap-tubes from the inside.

She took out the multitool.

She broke the paint seal on the upper hinge with the multitool's small flat blade. She broke the paint seal on the lower hinge. The seals had been laid in 1924 and last topped in 1986 and should not break easily. They did not. By eleven at night she had the upper seal broken. By midnight she had the lower seal broken.

She set the multitool down. She stood. She put her shoulder against the door at the level of the upper hinge.

She pushed.

The door rocked outward by a quarter inch and stopped.

She shifted her shoulder to the lower hinge. She pushed.

The door rocked outward by another quarter inch.

She shifted to the center. She pushed.

The door swung outward by three inches and stopped against the bolt on the outside.

She put her face to the gap.

The corridor outside the door was lit by the residual light of the stairwell. The emergency lights were on, but dim.

The bolt on the outside of the door was visible through the gap. It was a half-inch brass slide-bolt set in a brass keep. The keep was screwed to the brick of the wall outside the door with two slotted brass screws.

She put the chisel through the gap and against the screw heads.

By three eleven the screws were out. The keep was loose against the brick. She put pressure on the door. The bolt slid in the keep. The keep fell off the brick. The bolt fell to the corridor floor with a sound she would have heard from the head of the stairs at any time on any of the past eleven days.

The door fell open.

The corridor was empty. She did not go up to the corridor.

She went back down to the cold-treatment room and lifted the file box and brought it up. She set her field bag on top of the file box. She put away the chisel and the multitool in the field bag. She secured the bolt keep and the screws in an envelope and then placed it in the field bag because they were evidence and she was not leaving them on the corridor floor.

She walked up the stairs to the foyer.

The foyer was sixty-one. The chapel-corridor was forty-six. She did not stop. She walked through the front door of the central administration onto the portico and across the gravel to the Outback.

It was three eleven in the morning.

The Outback was where she had parked it on the morning of Day 11, at the foot of the four shallow steps of the portico. She opened the back. The hard drive was in the foam-lined case under the second tripod. The hard drive was a four-terabyte external drive she had bought in 2022 and had been backing up to nightly from the laptop, which meant the hard drive had every photograph she had taken on this contract plus every field-notebook page she had photographed at the end of every working day, plus the dossier from the state archive and the digital scan of the on-grounds cemetery ledger.

She brought the hard drive into the field office.

The field office at three sixteen was fifty-eight. She turned the heated vest up to high. She sat in the camp chair. She opened the laptop. She plugged the hard drive into the laptop. She opened the file box.

She took pictures of the forty-one photographs in the file box one at a time, each on the bare floorboards of the field office under the south window, the headlamp on full, the Pentax on the tripod. She photographed each one face-up and then face-down. The handwriting on the back of each was either Theodore Kessler's on the older photographs or Wendell Kessler's on the newer ones. The date written on the back was the date the photograph had been taken.

The eighty-two new stills imported. She named the folder MARSTON_HILL_BASEMENT_FILE_BOX.

She added the field notebook pages from Day 9. She added the eighty-two pictures of the photographs in the file box. She added the original eight stills of the Pemberton 1924 form from Day 5 and the eight from Day 7 and the forty-six stills of the East Wing chamber from Day 8 morning. She added the forensic team's Day 8 photographs which Owens had given her access to on Day 9 with Park's authorization. She added the Day 9 records-room inventory.

She compressed the folder. She uploaded it to two cloud accounts that did not share infrastructure.

The upload took, on the field office's cellular hotspot at three forty-one in the morning, twenty-eight minutes.

The upload completed at four oh nine.

She wrote three emails.

The first was to Park. The subject line was: *Marston Hill Day 12, 04:09. Contents of basement file box plus chain documentation.* The body was three sentences. The link to both cloud folders was at the bottom.

The second was to her editor at the Journal of American Historical Preservation. The subject line was: *Marston Hill closure-eve survey. Material in cloud folders linked. Hold publication; in process with state police.* The body was four sentences.

The third was to herself. The subject line was: *MARSTON HILL DAY 12 04:09 ARCHIVE LINKS.* The body was the two cloud links.

She sent the three emails at four eleven.

She closed the laptop. She put the hard drive in the foam-lined case. She put the field notebook in the side pocket. She put the file box on the floor by the camp chair, hasp open, photographs visible.

She stood and walked across the rear corridor. She did not stop.

She walked through the front door of the central administration onto the portico.

The eastern sky was the sky of a November morning thirty minutes before sunrise. It wasn't light yet. The wreckers' equipment on the access road was the silhouette of the wreckers' equipment against the not-yet-light sky.

Wendell Kessler was on the path between the portico and the trailer.

He had his hands in the pockets of his barn coat. He had no thermos this morning. The early light was just behind him putting his face in shadow.

He had been waiting.

He took a step forward as Kate came down the four shallow steps.

"Welton," he said. "I came to help you finish documenting. Dad would have wanted it."

She stopped on the bottom step.

She had her hand in the pocket of her field jacket. The phone in the pocket was already dialing Park because she had pressed the side-key three times on the way out of the building.

"I know what your father did," she said. "I know what you do."

He smiled.

He did not move his hands out of his pockets.

The smile was the same smile from Day 2 at the gate and Day 4 at the trailer and Day 5 at the trailer after Owens left and the Day 10 portico smile that had not been a smile.

The early light came up by a degree behind him. His face was still in shadow. His shadow on the gravel was longer than he was.

In her field-jacket pocket the phone vibrated once, which was the pattern the phone made when a call connected, and Park's voice came through the speaker she had cupped in her palm against her ribs:

"Welton. I'm hearing this. I'm hearing this. Hold on. We'll be there soon."

CHAPTER SIXTEEN

The hydrotherapy room

Day 12 · morning

"He did not love you, that's why he killed you."
— Daphne du Maurier, *Rebecca* (1938)

He took his right hand out of the barn coat pocket.

The hand had Eleanor Ross's old set of keys in it. The keys were on a brass ring with a brass tag that read in Eleanor's careful pre-1994 hand RESIDENT NURSE KEYS — DO NOT REMOVE FROM PROPERTY. Eleanor had not removed the keys from the property in 1994 because Eleanor had not been asked to. Wendell had taken the keys at some point in the eighties or nineties from Eleanor's office desk, the way a man with the run of the building took a thing he intended to keep. Wendell had kept the keys for thirty-one years.

He took his left hand out of the barn coat pocket.

The hand had a service revolver, a Smith & Wesson Model 10 in blued steel, four-inch barrel, the kind of revolver a state-hospital medical director had been issued in the early seventies for the safe in the medical director's office and had not been required to return at retirement in 1994 because the state had lost track of the fact it had ever been issued. The revolver was Theodore Kessler's.

It was not pointed at her.

He held it at his side, at the height of his hip, the muzzle down, the way a man carried a revolver he wanted to be able to raise without making the gesture of raising.

"Welton," he said. "Inside."

She did not move.

"The basement," he said. "We're going to the basement. You are going to walk in front of me at a measured pace, with your hands at your sides. Don't put your hands in your pockets. Don't turn. Walk to the door of the central administration and through the foyer to the rear corridor to the stairs to the lower level and down the stairs to the steel door of the hydrotherapy basement."

"Fine."

"Now, start talking about what you think you know."

He stepped aside on the path. She walked past him toward the portico. The phone in her field-jacket pocket was dialed to Park, and Park had her on the line.

She walked at a measured pace.

"I documented forty-one photographs from the basement file box this morning," she said.

"Did you?"

"On the SD card in the Pentax, on the laptop's hard drive, on the external drive in the field office, and on two cloud accounts."

"And?"

"Park has the cloud links."

"I assumed he would."

"You're stopping a witness."

"I'm stopping a witness, yes."

"There are other witnesses."

"There are. Eleanor is eighty-one and will not testify. Tessa is twenty-six and wasn't at the institution in any of the relevant years. Owens is a state employee whose chain of custody on the Day 8 chamber I've already had counsel review for technical defects. Park is competent but the case will be slower than the press will let it be. The press will lose interest by the time the case opens. I'll plead to a number of charges that are less than the charges I'd plead to if the witness who walked the building for fourteen days was available to testify to what she found in a file box on the morning of Day 12."

She came up the four shallow steps of the portico. She opened the front door of the central administration. She walked through the door into the foyer. She walked through the foyer into the rear corridor.

The chapel-corridor on her left was at forty-six. She did not look at it.

She walked past the records room. She walked past the field office. She came to the stairs at the south end of the rear corridor.

"Stop," he said.

She stopped at the top of the stairs.

He came up behind her and stood at a distance of five feet.

"Welton?"

"Yes."

"The next thing you're going to do is take the keys out of my right hand and unlock the steel door at the bottom of the stairs."

He held the keys out.

She took them out of his hand. She did not look at his face.

She walked down the upper flight of the staircase to the half-landing. She turned at the half-landing. She walked down the lower flight of the staircase to the steel door at the bottom of the lower level.

The steel door was open.

She had left it open at three eleven that morning. She had left her field bag with the keep and bolt on the floor of the corridor.

He came down the stairs behind her.

"Welton?"

"Yes."

"In."

She walked through the open door into the cold-treatment room.

She kept her hand on the doorframe as she went through. The doorframe was 1924 brick on 1924 mortar. She had been counting structural failures in this building since Day 8. The 1924 brick was the original load-bearing on this side of the lower level. The 1924 mortar was lime mortar, which had never been re-pointed. The doorframe was holding the lintel above the doorframe. The lintel above the doorframe was a steel I-beam set in the brick at construction.

The lintel had a hairline crack across the underside.

She had photographed the crack on Day 7 when she had walked the basement with the borescope and had marked it on her field map of the lower level for inclusion in the structural-condition report she would have filed on Day 13.

The crack was not a structural failure yet.

The crack was a structural failure waiting to happen, which was the kind of crack a preservation architect on her seventh closure-eve learned to read as a margin she could use.

She walked through the cold-treatment room into the shock-treatment room. She walked through the shock-treatment room into the basin room. She walked through the basin room into the duty room.

The duty room was empty. The recessed cabinet was open. The file box was not in the cabinet.

"Where is it," he said.

"In the field office."

"Where in the field office."

"On the floor by the camp chair."

He stood in the doorway of the duty room. He had the revolver at his hip. He had the keys back in his right hand because she had given them back at the bottom of the stairs without looking at his face.

"Sit down," he said.

She did not sit down.

She stood with her back to the duty desk and her hand at her side and the phone at her ribs continued to feed Park whatever Park would be able to hear.

"Welton?"

"Yes."

"Sit down."

"You will use the revolver if you decide to use the revolver. Not because I sat down or because I didn't sit down. I'm going to keep standing."

"Fine."

He smiled the third smile of the morning.

She decided to push, "What was the cabinet for."

"The cabinet was for the file box. The file box was for the photographs. You wouldn't understand. I like to remember them."

"I don't understand."

"The cabinet has a second compartment behind the first. It contains something I've been using since 1989 in the wing chair on Howard Street."

"Open it."

"You don't give orders in this room."

"I want to understand. Open it."

He paused.

He took half a step forward into the duty room.

Above his head the lintel above the duty-room doorway was a 1924 steel I-beam with a hairline crack across its underside. The crack was in the line of the beam directly above the spot Wendell now occupied.

The beam had been holding a corner of the chapel-corridor floor since 1924. The beam had taken the storm of Day 5. The beam had taken the dropping of three roof tiles in the West Wing slate failure which had loaded the chapel-corridor's lateral truss at an angle the truss had not been designed for. The beam had taken Voss's saw on Day 8 morning at a frequency that had carried through the brick of the East Wing partition and through the chapel-corridor's lath and into the lintel.

The crack in the underside of the lintel had widened by a degree on the evening of Day 8. She had photographed it on Day 9 morning before the records-room inventory.

The crack was at the limit of its structural margin.

Wendell shifted his weight onto his right foot inside the duty-room doorway.

The lintel went.

The lintel went in two pieces. The first piece was the half above the duty-room doorway. The second piece was the half above the chapel-corridor stair. The first piece dropped onto Wendell where he stood in the doorway. The second piece dropped the chapel-corridor floor a foot behind him. The chapel-corridor floor cracked along the line of the lintel and dropped six inches.

A spray of plaster and mortar dust came down. A piece of the plaster at the chapel-corridor end of the lintel struck Wendell on the shoulder. A larger piece struck him on the side of the head.

He went down.

The revolver hit the floor of the duty-room doorway.

She stepped past him.

She did not pick up the revolver or the keys. She was not going back into the duty room.

She ran.

Through the basin room, through the shock-treatment room, through the cold-treatment room, she ran. Up the lower flight of the staircase to the half-landing, turn, up the upper flight of the staircase to the rear corridor.

She ran past the chapel-corridor and through the records-room corridor and into the foyer and through the foyer onto the portico.

The eastern sky was light now, but the sun wasn't up yet. The wreckers' equipment on the access road was in silhouette against the eastern sky. The trooper's vehicle at the gate was at the gate. She saw a trooper at the gate on the radio.

Behind her in the central administration, the lintel of the chapel-corridor's main beam, which had been weakened by a hundred and two years of paint and a five-day nor'easter and a Day 8 saw and a Day 12 morning failure, gave.

The chapel-corridor floor between the central administration and the detached chapel went into the lower level in a piece. The chapel-corridor's roof followed the floor. The chapel-corridor's wall followed the roof.

The west wing's roof, which had been compromised since the '96 storm and which had been further compromised by the storm of Day 5 and which was held only by the truss above the morgue, took the lateral shock from the chapel-corridor's collapse and gave.

The west wing's slate roof came down into the morgue.

She was on the gravel by the time the dust reached the portico.

Two state-police vehicles were at the gate. The vehicles cleared the gate and stopped at the equipment line. Four troopers got out. Beasley was one of them. He came forward at a run.

"Welton."

She was panting, "Wendell. In the duty room of the hydrotherapy basement. Lintel down on him.

Revolver on the floor of the doorway. He was alive when I left him."

"Is anyone else inside."

"No."

"Is the building stable."

"No."

He turned to the other three. He pointed at one and said: "Stay with her." He pointed at the other two and said: "With me. The basement at the south end of the lower level. Call for fire and ambulance."

He went into the building.

She stood on the gravel beside the trooper who had been told to stay with her. The trooper was Jensen, twenty-five and not yet patient. He did not speak to her. He stood with his shoulder turned toward her and his eyes on the front door of the central administration.

The dust over the central administration was the color of old brick.

Behind the central administration the chapel sat where it had sat since 1873. The chapel-corridor between the chapel and the central administration was no longer between them.

The west wing's slate roof had come down into the morgue. The morgue was where Kate and Ray had found the femur on Day 4. The morgue had given up the femur. It had now given up its roof.

The east wing was intact.

The chamber on the second floor of the east wing was intact.

The records room was intact.

The field office was intact.

The file box was on the floor of the field office by the camp chair, hasp open, the photographs visible, where she had left it at four eleven.

In her field-jacket pocket the phone vibrated three times, which was the pattern the phone made when a call ended. Park had been on the line for eleven minutes. He had been on the line for the entire confrontation.

Park had heard.

Three people approached Beasley at the foot of the four shallow steps of the portico. Beasley had been inside for three minutes and was now back out and was on the radio. Wendell Kessler was walking with a trooper on each elbow at the pace of a man who had been struck on the side of the head by a plaster fragment from a lintel that had been holding for a hundred and two years and had stopped holding at six fifty-two on the morning of November eighth.

"He tried to run," the trooper told Beasley.

Wendell Kessler was conscious. He had a cut at the right temple that was bleeding into his right eye.

Beasley took Wendell Kessler at the foot of the portico steps. He walked Wendell Kessler at a slow pace across the gravel to the cone perimeter at the gate. He put Wendell Kessler in the back of the second state-police vehicle and closed the door.

Behind Kate the building of Marston Hill State Hospital, which had been built in 1873 by Edmund Caldwell as a model Kirkbride and which had been compromised at every load-bearing seam over a hundred and fifty-three years and which had defended its witness on the morning of November eighth at six fifty-two, settled.

She stood still.

She closed her eyes for a minute.

She opened them.

The field notebook came out of the side pocket of her field jacket. She took the pencil out of the inside pocket. She opened the notebook to the first blank page. She wrote:

Day 12, 06:52. Marston Hill central administration: chapel-corridor floor, roof, and wall: collapse. West wing slate roof: collapse into morgue. East wing: intact. Chamber on 2-E: intact. Records room: intact. Field office: intact. File box on floor of field office, photographs accessible. Subject W. Kessler in custody at gate. Service revolver and key ring on duty-room floor. Approx. eleven minutes of phone audio of confrontation forwarded to Park at 06:42 via emergency call. Forty-one photographs and chain documentation in two cloud accounts since 04:09. Building has, in its way, defended its witness.

She closed the notebook.

ARCHIVE EXCERPT

From Eleanor Ross's notebook · transcribed by her granddaughter · undated

I always knew about Theo. I never said. I had three children to feed and the home was my paycheck, and Theo was the medical director and he signed my evaluations every year. The boy was worse than the father from sixteen on. I caught him once on the women's ward at night when he had no business there, and I logged it as a duty round. I could have stopped one of them and I did not. I am writing this down so my granddaughter knows. Somebody should know who it was.

CHAPTER SEVENTEEN

Survival

Day 13

"Definitions belonged to the definers, not the defined."
— Toni Morrison, *Beloved* (1987)

She slept four hours.

The motel had been an option. The motel was forty-one miles south. Park had said drive south. Park had said it twice. But the Outback was sixty-two and she had a lap blanket and a folded tarp and extra batteries for the heated vest, and the motel was forty-one miles of remnant road in the dust of a partial collapse, and she could only afford four hours.

She moved all of her equipment to one side of the back where the seats were already folded down and anything that wouldn't fit went up to the front passenger seat. She set the tarp over the equipment and the laid flat seats, laid down with the heated vest on medium under the lap blanket, the field jacket folded under her head, and her boots at her feet.

She did not sleep at first.

Beasley was at the gate. The two state-police vehicles were at the gate. The fire crew was at the south end of the gravel lot, where the duty room had been opened and the lintel had been removed and Wendell Kessler had been carried out at seven thirty and taken in the second of the two state-police vehicles to the regional hospital under guard. The fire crew was finishing the stabilization of the chapel-corridor's collapse and had said the stabilization was good enough to leave for today.

She slept at ten.

By two she was up. She was up and on the trailer step with a cup of bad coffee from the trailer thermos and the field notebook open. At three she was at the regional state-police barracks in town, in the same eight-by-ten interview room she had been in on the morning of Day 10. Park was across from her with two folders, a recorder, and a junior detective whose name she filed as Daoud and a cup of black coffee he refilled twice in the first hour.

The statement took five hours.

She gave it in the order the work had unfolded: Day 1 to Day 12. She gave it from the field notebook on her lap, page by page, with the dates and the times marked. She did not edit. She did not summarize. She did not adjust for the audience. She told it as an architect would, noting the specific structural and atmospheric measurements she had observed. It was how she would tell anything she had logged at any closure-eve site in twenty years.

Park did not interrupt. Daoud did not interrupt. The recorder ran.

When the statement was done at eight Park asked her to stay for an identification.

"The forensic team has aged the chair-chamber remains and run the surviving file fragments. They won't be ready with a final identification for another week. The provisional is solid. I'm going to read you the provisional and ask whether the provisional matches what you expected."

He opened the second folder.

"Patient: Alice Margaret Pemberton, born June nineteenth, 1925, in the institution. Committed at sixteen, in 1941, by the order of the medical director who had succeeded Edmund Caldwell, with no next of kin signing. Cause of death not established. Date of death estimated by skeletal evidence as approximately the late nineteen-fifties to early sixties, which would have made her in her thirties at death. Provisional. There is a half-sheet of intake paperwork that survived in the East Wing chamber with the body, and the half-sheet is consistent."

"Alice Pemberton the second."

"Yes."

"Daughter of the 1924 Alice."

"Yes."

"Born inside the institution. Raised in the children's annex. Committed at sixteen as her mother's daughter. Never discharged. Held in a chair in a chamber on the second floor of the women's wing of the building she had been born in. Named at last on a Monday a hundred years after her mother went in."

"That is the provisional."

She shook her head and did not say anything for the count of three.

"Park."

"Yes."

"Thank you for reading it to me."

"I read it because you are the survey supervisor on the chain of custody and you are entitled to know it."

"Okay."

A small smile, "I would have read it to you anyway."

She returned it, "Thank you."

He closed the folder.

"The contemporary cavity held Beth Carrow. We had her at the visual on Day 10."

"Right."

"Welton."

"Yes."

"I was going to ask you not to be on the property tomorrow morning before nine."

"I have to be on the property tomorrow at six."

"You have to be on the property tomorrow at six?"

A nod, "The wreckers."

"You are the survey supervisor. The contract runs through tomorrow at the end of the day. The state has decided to proceed with demolition on schedule. I have made my position known to them, but the state has decided."

"You don't agree."

"No. But, the state decided anyway, over my objections. The east wing's second floor is being lifted intact under tarp for evidentiary preservation. The chapel-corridor is already down. The west wing's roof is already down. The rest of the building goes tomorrow on schedule."

"Okay."

"I'll have a trooper at the gate at four. Beasley, if you want him."

"I want him, thank you."

"Welton?"

"Yes."

"You did your job."

"I did some of it."

"You did your job."

She walked out at eight forty-one. Daoud held the door. The press was on the road outside the barracks. There were three trucks. There were two cameras at the corner of the lot. There was a woman with a microphone at the foot of the steps. The press did not have her name yet because Park had not given it. The press would have it by midnight from the demolition contractor's payroll.

She headed to Marston Hill. She drove to the Cedarwood instead at the last bend in the road, parked at the side of the building where the front desk could not see her car, and went into Room 14 and ate a microwave thing the front-desk woman had left in the freezer, and she called Joanne.

Joanne picked up on the second ring.

"Kate."

"Joanne." She filled her in on the last two days events.

Then, "Is it on the news there yet."

"It will be by midnight."

"It is on the news here."

"Mom is having a clear hour. The residence called me an hour ago. They asked if I wanted to come over for it. I'm driving over now."

"Put me on the phone with her when you get there."

"I will."

"Joanne."

"Yes."

"I'm driving south on the morning of the eleventh. I'll be with her by the evening. The contract ends tomorrow."

"On the eleventh. I'll meet you at the residence."

"Okay."

"I'm driving. Kate, just pulling into the lot. I'm going up. I'll hand her the phone in three minutes."

"Alright."

"Kate."

"Yes."

"I love you."

"I love you too."

Joanne did not put the call on hold. The phone was in Joanne's pocket, by the rustle. The phone went up the stairs and down a corridor. A door opened. A door closed. Joanne said, *Mom, I have Kate on the phone.* Margaret said, *Oh.* The phone came up to a face.

"Kate."

"Mom."

"Kate."

"Mom."

It was Margaret's voice from 2018. The librarian's careful rhythm. The slight dryness at the end of each sentence. The voice of a woman who had been alive for seventy-one years and who had at this hour of the day been given back to herself by a strange neurology no one understood yet.

"Kate, please come home."

"I'm coming."

"On the eleventh, Joanne said."

"On the eleventh. I'll drive south on the morning of the eleventh. I'll be there in the late evening."

"Drive safely."

"I will."

"Kate?"

"Yes."

"I'm sorry I haven't been well."

"Mom. There is nothing to be sorry for."

"There is. I'm sorry."

"Okay, Mom."

A pause.

"Kate?"

"Yes."

"It is a hard thing, what is happening to me."

"I know."

"I'm not always well. I'm okay right now."

"I know."

"Kate, please come home."

"I'm coming."

"On the eleventh."

"On the eleventh."

"Yes."

"I love you, Mom."

"I love you too, sweetheart."

Joanne came back on. "Kate, she's tired now."

Kate said, 'I'll be at the site at six tomorrow morning. Call me tonight before five if you can."

"I will."

They hung up.

Kate sat on the edge of the bed. She did not turn the lamp on. She did not call Tessa Ross. She did not call Park. She did not call her editor at the Journal of American Historical Preservation, who had read the cloud links at four eleven that morning and had emailed her at six asking what to do with them.

She did not cry.

She would, in the late evening of Day 14 at a different motel ninety miles south. She would not cry tonight. There was a Day 14 between her and the crying, and the Day 14 was a building coming down on a schedule she had walked for fourteen days and had photographed one elevation at a time, and the Day 14 work was demolition.

She set the alarm for four.

She turned out the lamp.

CHAPTER EIGHTEEN

The wreckers

Day 14 · morning

"I came to explore the wreck."
— Adrienne Rich, *Diving into the Wreck* (1973)

She was at the gate at five fifty-three.

Beasley raised it. Beasley was at hour zero of his second twelve hour shift in three days. He was patient because his wife had told him Park had asked for him by name.

"Welton."

"Beasley."

"The wreckers' equipment is staged on the access road behind you. The first cut is at nine."

"Okay."

"Welton."

"Yes."

"My condolences."

"Beasley."

"Yes."

"I'm not the one to give them to."

"No. But you're the one I'm with."

She drove through.

The gravel lot at six was empty of crew. The trailer was dark. Ray's truck was in the lot and Ray wasn't in the truck. Ray was on the four shallow steps of the portico of the central administration with a thermos and two enamel cups beside him.

He poured her one as she came up.

She took the cup. She sat on the step beside him. The November dawn had not come up over the walnut crowns yet. The eastern sky was the color of the inside of a shell again.

"I read the news," he said.

"I figured."

"You're alright."

"I'm alright."

He paused, "You're not."

"No."

A pause.

"The state is going through with the demolition," he said.

"I know."

"As the foreman of record. I have to run the demolition when they tell me."

"I know."

"I don't agree."

"Okay."

"I'm running it because the state makes the contracts and I have the next contract from the state in February. The state pays my crew, and the crew has houses they have to live in. I'd like you to know that I'm running it because it is required and not because I agree."

"Ray."

"Yes."

"I know you're running it because it is required. I have not, for twelve days, thought you were running it because you agreed with anything."

"Good."

"I don't agree either."

"I know."

"I have put my disagreement on the record. I've sent it to the preservation registry. I've copied my editor at the Journal of American Historical Preservation. The disagreement will be on file. The disagreement won't stop the demolition."

"No."

He poured her a second cup.

The wreckers came up the access road at seven. The cut crew came in at seven thirty. The county fire department came in at seven forty-five and parked their two units inside the equipment line. The state evidence team came in at eight and went directly to the east wing's second floor with the contract for the lift. The state evidence team had a thirty-foot flatbed and a crane and a tarp and a license number that did not appear on any state-licensed-facility registry because the state evidence team was its own thing.

At eight thirty, Eleanor Ross arrived at the gate.

Tessa drove the car. Eleanor was in the front passenger seat with a wheelchair folded in the back. She parked at the cone perimeter. Tessa got out, unfolded the wheelchair, and came around to the passenger side and helped Eleanor out of the car and into the chair.

Beasley raised the gate.

Tessa wheeled Eleanor in. Tessa wheeled the chair to the foot of the four shallow steps of the portico and stopped where the gravel was firm. Eleanor was wrapped in a blanket. She was wearing the same pre-1994 hospital cardigan she had been wearing in her armchair on Day 6. Her hands were folded on her lap and were shaking by a small amount that was not the cold.

Kate came down the four shallow steps.

"Eleanor."

"Kate."

"I'm glad you came."

"I came because Tessa told me I should come. I don't remember why."

"That's okay, I do."

A pause.

"Tessa," Kate said, "would you go to the trailer for a moment. There is a thermos on the step with three cups."

Tessa nodded and walked to the trailer.

Kate crouched beside the wheelchair the way she had crouched beside Eleanor's armchair on the morning of Day 6. She put a hand on the arm of the chair.

"Eleanor."

"Yes."

"You told me on Day 6 not to go into the hydrotherapy basement alone."

"I don't remember telling you."

"You told me. You took my wrist. You said you knew in the morning and you had not written it down before you forgot. You said you were sorry."

"Oh."

"I went into the basement on Day 11. I came out on Day 12. The state arrested Wendell Kessler at the gate on Day 12. He is in the regional hospital. He will be in custody through trial. The case against him will hold up. The chain of custody will hold up."

"Kate?"

"Yes."

"I don't remember Wendell Kessler."

"That's okay."

"I knew his father."

"You did."

"I knew his father did not cross the lines I could see."

"Yes."

"There was something I wasn't telling you."

"You told me. You told me by way you told it. You told me everything you could tell me and wrote the rest down for Tessa."

"Did I?"

"You did."

She did not let go of the arm of the chair. She did not need to let go of the arm of the chair. Eleanor's hand came up off her lap and onto Kate's hand on the arm of the chair and stayed there.

Tessa came back from the trailer with the cups.

She poured and handed a cup to Eleanor. Eleanor's free hand took the cup.

Tessa handed a cup to Kate. Kate's free hand took the cup.

She handed the third cup to Ray, who had come up from the equipment line and stood beside her.

The wreckers' first cut was at nine.

The first cut was the west wing's southwest corner, the corner that had been failing since the '96 storm and had taken the lateral collapse on Day 12. The excavator's grapple came down on the corner of the slate roof that had survived the Day 12 collapse and pulled it off the wall in a single piece. The slate came down. The brick came down behind the slate. The dust rose in a column above the gravel lot and crossed the lot at the height of the chapel roof.

Eleanor watched.

Her hand on Kate's hand did not move.

The grapple came back. The grapple took the second corner of the west wing. The brick came down. The wood frame behind the brick came down. The slate roof in pieces came down on the wood frame.

Eleanor's eyes were on the building. Eleanor's eyes had been lucid this morning, but were now questioning why she was there. But, her eyes did not move. Her hand did not move.

A tear came down the right side of Eleanor's face.

The tear was on the cheekbone where Eleanor had a small mole Kate had not noticed on Day 6. It came down the cheek and stopped on the line of her jaw where it sat and did not go any further because Eleanor wasn't warm enough for a tear to go further than her jaw line.

Eleanor did not wipe the tear. She did not know about the tear.

Kate did not wipe the tear either. It was a sad witness to the underlying knowledge that was lost somewhere between the neurons of Eleanor's brain.

The west wing came down at nine forty-three. The chapel-corridor's remaining structure, which had been hanging since Day 12, came down at ten oh six in sympathy with the west wing's loss of the lateral truss. The chapel itself, which had been the chapel since 1873, which had not been entered since Day 7, which had taken the wind through its broken sash on Day 5, and the sound of a person breathing on the evening of Day 5, was the third major structure to come down. It came down at ten forty-one.

The four of them watched the chapel come down.

The state evidence team lifted the second floor of the east wing in a piece. The lift was a thing that took thirty minutes. The flatbed pulled out of the gate at eleven oh four with the chamber and the cavity and the corridor between them under tarp.

Eleanor watched the flatbed leave.

"Kate?"

"Yes."

"That was the women's wing?"

"Yes."

"They are going to her?"

"Yes."

The rest of the east wing came down at noon. The administration building came down at twelve forty-five. By one the central administration was rubble in piles, sorted by the demolition crew into what would go to landfill and what would go to the state's evidence yard. By one, the cemetery, which the state archaeology unit would work in November and December, was the only thing of Marston Hill State Hospital that remained above grade.

Eleanor's hand was still on Kate's hand.

Tessa said, "Granny, we should go."

Eleanor said, "Yes, Tessa-pet."

Tessa wheeled the chair back toward the car.

Kate walked with them as far as the gate.

At the gate Eleanor put her hand up.

Kate stopped. Tessa stopped.

Eleanor turned the chair by an inch with her good hand. She looked back at the gravel lot and the rubble and the dust on the rubble and the equipment in the lot and the cone perimeter and the state troopers at the trailer and Beasley at the gate and Ray at the access road with his crew taking down the equipment line.

She said, "I don't know why I cried."

Kate said, "I know."

She patted Kate's hand one more time.

Tessa wheeled her to the car.

CHAPTER NINETEEN

What comes out

Day 14 · afternoon

"After great pain, a formal feeling comes — The Nerves sit ceremonious, like Tombs —"
— Emily Dickinson, *Poem 372* (c. 1862)

The first afternoon cavity opened at one fifty-eight.

Ray's crew had been working on the rubble of the chapel since eleven, which followed the order on the cut foreman's protocol. It was last among the standing structures, but the chapel rubble was first among the cleared pieces. The chapel was the smallest and on the cemetery side of the property. The chapel was the structure the state archaeology unit would be working on in November and December, and Ray's crew was clearing the rubble of the chapel down to the slab so the archaeology unit had a clean hand-off.

At one fifty-eight, Marcus, who had been on Ray's crew for eight years, called out from the chapel slab. He did not sound panicked. On his second asylum job in 2003 he saw a bone in a wall and had not forgotten it. He did not raise his voice. He raised his hand. He called Ray by name.

Ray came over. They stood at the back of the chapel slab where the chapel's east wall had stood until ten forty-one. The chapel's east wall had been a brick wall on a brick foundation that had gone three feet below grade and taken the lateral pressure of the slate roof for a hundred and fifty-three years. Marcus's grapple had come down on the foundation and had pulled three feet of brick from below grade. Behind the brick had been a cavity the size of a coffin laid lengthwise. Inside the cavity had been a body.

Kate came up at two oh four.

The state evidence team was already on the slab. The state evidence team had been on the gravel lot since the lift of the east wing's second floor and had not left. Owens was not on the slab; Owens was at the state lab with the chair-chamber remains. Hector was on the slab. Hector had come on after Ray's call at one fifty-nine and had been on the slab at two oh one with a kit and three technicians and the same fold-up table from Day 8.

The body in the cavity behind the chapel's east wall was a woman.

She was wrapped in what had been a wool blanket which had turned the brown-black of wool a hundred years buried. The body was small, by the visible bone. The body had been in the cavity since approximately the date the cavity had been built, which by Hector's preliminary estimation was the early nineteen-thirties, when the chapel's east wall had been re-pointed and the foundation course replaced after a spring flood.

There was a half-sheet of paper folded inside the wool blanket against the woman's chest. It was a folded square the size of a hand. The half-sheet was, Hector said, possibly an intake form. It was dated nineteen thirty-one.

Kate did not ask Hector to unfold it. Hector would unfold it at the state lab under sterile conditions with the respect deserved for a hundred-year-old institutional intake form folded against the chest of a woman who had been put behind a foundation of brick by a person who had wanted the form to stay with her.

The half-sheet had been put there by a person.

That was the line of thought Kate was holding now.

She photographed the cavity at two oh nine. She photographed the wool blanket at two ten. She photographed the half-sheet of paper at two eleven. She photographed the brick of the foundation at two twelve. She photographed the spalled corner of the foundation block where the grapple had come through at two thirteen.

She wrote in the field notebook:

Chapel slab, east wall foundation, 14:09. Cavity behind 1932-era foundation. Adult female remains, wool blanket, half-sheet intake form folded against chest. Form ink dated 1931. Photographed in place by me, then by Hector. Extraction by state forensic team. Body labeled provisional A2 pending lab.

She closed the notebook.

The second afternoon cavity opened at two thirty-six.

The second cavity was on the east side, beneath the women's-wing service stair. The women's-wing service stair had been the stair Kate had marked on Day 2 with blue masking tape against the plaster where the 1923 rebuild had walled it off. The stair had been on the 1923 plan and not on the 1947 plan. It had been the first thing in the building that had not made architectural sense.

The crew had taken the women's wing apart from the second floor down. The second floor lift was already on a flatbed at the state evidence yard. The crew was now at the foundation level. The grapple came down on the southwest corner of the foundation, where the women's-wing service stair had ended in a small underground vault that had been below the floor of the basement. It had not been on any plan. The crew had not known about it until the grapple had come down.

The vault was eight feet by four. It contained two bodies.

The two bodies were both adult females. The two bodies looked historical, by the visible bone. They were laid head to foot in the only way two bodies could be laid in a vault eight feet by four. There was no blanket this time. The two bodies were on the foundation slab of the institution.

Hector came down off the chapel slab at two forty-one.

He set up a second table on the women's wing's foundation slab. He set up the lights. He gave two of the technicians to Marcus's crew on the chapel and kept one with him on the women's wing.

Kate stood at the foot of the foundation cut. She did not get into the cut. She did not need to. Hector waved her in for the chain-of-custody photograph. She took the chain-of-custody photograph of the two bodies in the vault.

The two bodies were, judging from the file fragments the state archive had pulled forward to her on Tuesday, possibly Estelle Doran and her sister-in-letter Marie Doran. Estelle had written to her sister

Beth in June 1961 from this institution and had said Marie was taken yesterday and had not come back. Marie had been the woman the letter had been about. Estelle and Marie had not been buried in the on-grounds cemetery. They had been, according to the surviving institutional ledger, *transferred — destination unrecorded* in July 1961.

Kate did not say this out loud at the foot of the foundation cut.

She said it later in the field notebook:

Women's wing foundation vault, beneath service stair, 14:36. Two adult female remains, head-to-foot. Provisional B1 and B2. Cross-ref against state archive 1961 transfers; possible Doran (E.) and Doran (M.). Verify with lab.

She took the photographs Hector asked her to take. She did not extract any body, touch any body, fold any blanket, or unfold any half-sheet. She did not, by three in the afternoon, have a job description that fit what she was doing.

She was no longer a documenter.

She was a witness.

The third afternoon cavity opened at three twenty-two.

The third cavity was in the north corner of the central administration's foundation slab, which had been exposed at twelve forty-five when the administration building had come down. The third cavity was the smallest of the afternoon cavities. It was the size of a child's bed.

The body in the third cavity was an adult female. It had no blanket and no paper. The position it was laid in the cavity suggested she had been alive when placed in it. This body had no file fragment that survived the institution.

The state archaeology unit, when it came in November and December, would run the bone against the state archive. The state archive's surviving record on the institution from 1873 to 1923 was a third of a list and two-thirds a series of empty pages and the half of a ledger that had been kept by Edmund Caldwell himself in handwriting that had degraded by the nineteen-eighties to a smudge against pulp. The archaeology unit would not, with the available evidence, find a name that matched.

The third body was, according to the state archive, no one.

Kate photographed the third cavity at three twenty-six. She photographed the foundation at three twenty-eight. She photographed the corner where the grapple had come through at three twenty-nine.

She wrote in the field notebook:

Central administration foundation, north corner, 15:22. Adult female remains, no blanket, no paper, no surviving institutional file fragment. Provisional C1. State archaeology unit (Nov-Dec) will run against pre-1923 surviving record. Probability of identification: low. Body to be received by state lab and held for possibility of family DNA submission.

She closed the notebook.

She did not know whether the building was finally giving up its dead, or whether the building was simply being forced to let go of it's secrets. She did not know whether the cavities had been found because the building, in coming down, had wanted them found, or whether the cavities had been found because the wreckers' grapple had been thorough.

She had decided she did not need to know.

By four the afternoon's count was three. By four the afternoon's count of the building's recovered women, across the full two weeks, was seven.

Patient: PEMBERTON, Alice Margaret (the elder), 1903–1931, intake 1924. Possible occupant of the chapel-slab cavity, by the half-sheet date.

Patient: PEMBERTON, Alice Margaret (the younger), 1925–c.1958, intake 1941. Confirmed occupant of the East Wing chamber, by Owens's provisional Day 13.

Patient: DORAN, Estelle, 1939–c.1961, intake 1959, transferred destination unrecorded 1961. Possible occupant of the women's-wing foundation vault.

Patient: DORAN, Marie, dates unknown, taken in June 1961 per Estelle's smuggled letter. Possible occupant of the women's-wing foundation vault.

Patient: BISHOP, Mary, 1925–1949, intake 1947, lobotomy 1948, on the file as *family removed remains, August 1949* though the family had not removed the remains. Possible occupant of one of the cavities yet to be ledgered.

Patient: SANDRA K., 23 in 1989, on the 1989 incident report. Possible recovery from the file box at the regional state-police evidence room, which the photograph Kate had filed on Day 11 had named her.

Patient: C1, no name, no file, no surviving paper. The third body in the third cavity. The unidentified.

Six named, provisionally. One unnamed.

Kate had decided, on the foundation slab of the women's wing at three forty-eight on the afternoon of Day 14, that the seven were the seven. She suspected that the unidentified woman would not be named in this lifetime and she had decided that the unidentified woman did not require her name to be a person who had been in this building. The witness function did not require completeness.

This incompleteness was acceptable.

She did not tell any of the troopers or the forensic technicians or Ray or Hector that she had decided this. The decision wasn't theirs to make. It was hers. Only she could decide what could be carried and what could not.

She went to the trailer at four twelve to make Hector a cup of coffee.

CHAPTER TWENTY

Evening

Day 14 · evening

"One must have a mind of winter To regard the frost and the boughs Of the pine-trees crusted with snow."
— Wallace Stevens, *The Snow Man* (1921)

She left Marston Hill at five eleven.

There was no light left. The walnut crowns on the access road were bare against the no-light. The wreckers' equipment was being moved out of the gravel lot by the demolition contractor's transport crew and was being staged on the access road for the morning move, except the cone perimeter, which was staying through the state archaeology unit's November-December work.

Beasley raised the gate one last time.

"Welton."

"Beasley."

"Park said to tell you he'll call you tomorrow."

"Alright."

"Welton?"

"Yes."

"What do you do next?"

She thought about it for a moment

"I'll drive south. I'll stop when I'm too tired to drive. Tonight, I'll write a report no one has asked me to write. Tomorrow, I'll drive the rest of the way to my mother in the morning.."

"That sounds about right."

"Thanks."

"Welton?"

"Yes."

"It was an honor."

She did not say anything right away.

Then, "Beasley."

"Yes."

"Likewise."

He raised the gate.

She drove through.

She had two things in the car. First, she had a single brick from the East Wing, taken from the rubble of the women's-wing second floor lift at four thirty by the state evidence team and given to her by Hector at four forty-five with the chain-of-custody form for a single brick from the East Wing of Marston Hill State Hospital. It was signed by Hector and countersigned by Park's deputy who had come up at four thirty to brief her on the Day 14 statement she would give in the morning. The brick was a 1923 brick, fired in the local kiln that had supplied the institution's reform-era reconstruction, eight inches by four by two and three quarters, weight, according to her field bag's small scale, four pounds seven ounces.

She also had the original 1924 intake form for Pemberton, Alice Margaret, signed out properly from the state archive into her preservation custody on the morning of Day 14 by an emergency protocol Park had countersigned at six. The intake form was in an archival sleeve in the laptop case. The intake form had been, by then, the most photographed piece of paper in the state's preservation registry and was on its way to a museum.

She drove south on the state highway.

The state highway went past the diner that was now an LLC operating under a name in a font nobody had bought since 1991. The diner was open. There was a single truck in the lot. She did not stop.

The state highway went past the supermarket where she had bought yellow flowers on the morning of Day 6. The supermarket was open. There were three cars in the lot. She did not stop.

The state highway went past the regional state-police barracks. There were no press trucks at the barracks at five thirty in the evening on a Tuesday. The press had moved on. The press had moved on by mid-afternoon when the wreckers had finished the building. The press would be back when the case opened. The case would open when Park completed the investigation. He would only call if finished when all of the evidence was complete and the lab completed its work. It would probably require the dig at the chapel and cemetery to finish.

She drove out of town on the south road.

The motel ninety miles south was a Days Inn at the Springfield exit. The Days Inn was three stories. At the front desk she paid in the cash she had from the state. She took the key. She went up to room two-oh-four, which was on the second floor at the south end of the building. She had asked for it when she had booked at six.

She set the field bag on the bed. She set the laptop on the kitchenette table. She set the brick on the windowsill, where the light from the parking lot would fall on it through the curtains. She set the archival sleeve with the Pemberton intake form on the kitchenette table beside the laptop.

She did not sleep.

She wrote.

She had been writing the report in her head for fourteen days. It was the report she had been composing on the afternoon of Day 4 when Owens had aged the femur in the morgue duct at a hundred years. She had not committed it to the page until the evening of Day 14 because she wanted to have all of the facts first.

The report had a paragraph for each of the seven women.

Alice Margaret Pemberton (the elder), 1903 to 1931, twenty-eight years old at the institution's recorded death and twenty-one at her husband's recorded committal, who had been at Bryn Mawr for two years before her husband had withdrawn her support and who had been at Marston Hill for seven years before the institution had recorded her death as exhaustion following infection and who had been, on the evidence of the chapel-slab cavity, possibly put in a corner of the foundation by a person who had wanted her intake form folded against her chest.

Alice Margaret Pemberton (the younger), 1925 to approximately 1958, born in the institution and raised in the children's annex and committed at sixteen as her mother's daughter and never discharged. She had been held in a chair in a chamber on the second floor of the women's wing of the building she had been born in.

Estelle Doran, 1939 to approximately 1961, who had written to her sister Beth in June 1961 from the institution and said Marie had been taken and she had not been heard from again.

Marie Doran, dates unknown, who had been taken in June 1961 and had not come back, and who was, according to the foundation vault, with Estelle.

Mary Bishop, 1925 to 1949, who had been lobotomized at twenty-three and had died at twenty-four and whose family had not removed her remains in August 1949 because the institution had not given them remains to remove.

Sandra K., twenty-three in 1989, who had been transferred to Ward 4-E for behavioral deterioration following a family visit and whose full name was not on the page because the page had not preserved her surname. She was, in the photograph in the basement file box, the woman in 1989 institutional dress with Theodore Kessler's pencil annotation on the back.

Finally, the unidentified woman in the third cavity, who had no surviving file fragment and whose name the state archaeology unit would, by the available evidence, not recover. The paragraph was the shortest of the seven. She was a person. She had been in this building. Her name wasn't required to acknowledge that. Kate would be a witness to her death, even if she never had a name.

The report was eleven pages.

She finished it at three eleven in the morning.

She emailed the report to her editor at the Journal of American Historical Preservation at three thirteen with a brief subject line that said *Marston Hill closure report — field-notebook accounting — not for publication without state-police clearance.* It was a subject line her editor would understand.

She emailed Tessa Ross at three nineteen. The subject line of that email said *Eleanor*. The body of that email was four sentences. She acknowledged that Eleanor had been at the gate for four hours and had been part of the demolition as the witness she had always been for the building. Kate promised she would write a longer letter after she had slept. Finally, she said Tessa was the future of the moral question Eleanor's notebook had left behind, and that the future was, in Kate's estimation, in good hands.

She closed the laptop.

EPILOGUE

The brick

Late November

"Your absence has gone through me like thread through a needle. Everything I do is stitched with its color."
— W. S. Merwin, *Separation* (1963)

The apartment in the assisted-living residence was on the ground floor on the south corridor. It was a one-bedroom unit with a window that looked out onto a lawn and a row of birch.

It was warm. The thermostat in the apartment was set to seventy-two by the residence and it was held at seventy-two regardless of the season. There was a recliner near the window and a windowsill beside the recliner with a stack of unread mail on it.

The brick was on the windowsill, holding down the stack of unread mail.

Margaret was in the recliner.

Today was a good day. The residence had said so when Kate had come at ten. They were right. Margaret was lucid. She had been lucid since about eight thirty. Margaret would, by the residence's three-week journal of clear hours, lose this clarity at around two in the afternoon and might or might not have it back tomorrow.

Margaret was looking at the morning paper, folded to the crossword. She had her glasses on and a pencil in her hand. Her white hair was pulled back in the clip Kate did not see most women her age wearing.

Kate sat in the chair beside the recliner.

The investigation was ongoing. Wendell Kessler had been charged with three murders and was being held without bail at the state's high-security forensic-psychiatric unit, which was a place his father had once visited as a state consultant. The state-level review of Theodore Kessler's tenure had been opened in late November. The review would take at least a year. It might end in posthumous decertification, which was something Kate had not heard of three months ago and which she now understood as the state's term for stripping a doctor's license after the doctor was dead. It did not punish as much as it acknowledged the victims and corrected the historical record.

The site at Marston Hill was now a fenced lot with a backhoe and a state evidentiary tent. The state archaeology unit was working the cemetery. They had not recovered a name for the woman in the third cavity yet. The state archaeology unit had recovered six surnames Kate had not entered in the report and which would be added to it when she revised in February. Kate had identified six of the seven bodies. The seventh was, according to the preliminary read, going to remain unnamed.

She had not been back to the property.

Her plan was to be back there in the spring, when the state preservation registry would convene a meeting at the site to mark the close of the historical-preservation contract with a small bronze plaque they had agreed to fund. They had asked Kate to draft the wording and she had. She had written forty-one words, and it was, when she read it aloud to the cat at her apartment in Hartford, the right length.

Margaret put down the crossword.

"Kate."

"Mom."

"It is a good day today."

"It is."

A pause.

Margaret looked at the window. The birch beyond the lawn were bare. The parking lot beyond the birch had, on this late-November morning, three cars and a delivery van. The delivery van was unloading what looked like a stack of folded boxes.

"That brick," Margaret said.

"Yes."

"Where did it come from."

"From the building I just finished closing."

"The asylum."

"Yes."

"The east wing."

"The east wing."

Margaret looked at the brick.

"Kate."

"Yes."

"I'm glad you came home."

She put her hand on her mother's hand.

"I am too."

The leaves outside the window had stopped falling. The leaves had stopped falling on the eighteenth, which had been a Wednesday, by the residence's groundskeeping log. They were the color of dead leaves starting to wear into the earth.

The brick on the windowsill held down the unread mail.

The unread mail held a letter from Tessa Ross that had come on the fifteenth, postmarked the twelfth from town, two pages by the thickness of the envelope. Kate had read the letter at the apartment in Hartford on the fifteenth. She said that Eleanor had been lucid on the day of the demolition and had not been fully lucid since. Eleanor was eating well, but had crying episodes, even though she did not know what she was sad about. Tessa promised to write again.

The letter was on her mother's windowsill in the assisted-living residence three states south because Kate had brought it with her to read out loud to her mother on a good day, and this was a good day. She would read it today.

Margaret returned to the crossword and picked up her pencil. She looked at a clue.

"Eight letters," she said. "Closure, comma, related to."

"Architectural?"

"It says comma related to."

Kate thought about it.

"Building?"

"Building has the right number of letters."

"What is the across."

Margaret read the across, but Kate did not know it. They worked the puzzle for a while.

The brick on the windowsill held down the unread mail. The mail held the letter from Tessa Ross. The letter was for later. The letter was for the part of the day a daughter could read a letter to a mother about a friend who was no longer fully herself. Her mother was, on a good day, fully herself. She had said *I'm glad you came home.*

She put her hand on her mother's hand a second time.

Her mother turned the hand over and held it with her own.

Outside the window the leaves on the lawn did not move.

Inside the apartment the thermostat held at seventy-two.

The brick was on the windowsill where the brick had been since Kate had set it down on the eleventh, the day she had come home, the day Margaret had been having a good morning in the recliner by the window and had said, *Oh, you brought me a paperweight.*

She said it like a woman who had been a high-school librarian for forty years, with full attention and the small dryness at the end of the sentence that was her signature.

The brick was a paperweight.

It was also a brick from the East Wing of Marston Hill State Hospital, which had stood from 1923 to two oh four on the afternoon of November tenth, 2026.

The brick was both.

Both was the answer. Both was, in Kate's estimation, the way she viewed her job. Both a documenter and a witness.

She could live with it.

The afternoon came.

She picked up the letter to read it to her mother.

www.ingramcontent.com/pod-product-compliance
Lightning Source LLC
LaVergne TN
LVHW010655110826
845149LV00014B/3110

9798988616580